AUDREY J. WHITSON

THE
DEATH
OF
ANNIE
THE
WATER
WITCHER
BY
LIGHTNING

NeWest Press

Library and Archives Canada Cataloguing in Publication
Whitson, Audrey J. (Audrey Joan), 1957–, author
The death of Annie the Water Witcher by lightning / Audrey J. Whitson.
Issued in print and electronic formats.
ISBN 978-1-988732-47-3 (softcover).
ISBN 978-1-988732-48-0 (epub).
ISBN 978-1-988732-49-7 (Kindle).
I. Title.
PS8645.H5688D43 2019   C813'.6   C2018-904512-4   C2018-904513-2

Board editor: Douglas Barbour
Book design: Natalie Olsen, Kisscut Design
Cover flowers © lisima/shutterstock.com
Author photo: Alana Whitson

NeWest Press acknowledges the Canada Council for the Arts, the Alberta Foundation for the Arts, and the Edmonton Arts Council for support of our publishing program. This project is funded in part by the Government of Canada. ¶ NeWest Press acknowledges that the land on which we operate is Treaty 6 territory and a traditional meeting ground and home for many Indigenous Peoples, including Cree, Saulteaux, Niitsitapi (Blackfoot), Métis, and Nakota Sioux.

#201, 8540–109 Street   Edmonton, Alberta   T6G 1E6
780.432.9427
NeWest Press   www.newestpress.com

No bison were harmed in the making of this book.
Printed and bound in Canada   1 2 3 4 5   21 20 19

For Theresa,

my mother, and first reader

I

ANNIE GALLAGHER

You can smell the rain on the wind, a right smell for witching. The aspen that survived have taken on a tawny-yellow cast, the way they colour just before the limbs awaken. The willow seem the stronger, most seem to have resisted the drought. Deeper roots maybe. The black poplar, nothing but grey weathered sticks punctuating the pale green understory. You can see it in the shelter belts, the thinning this year, the trees that just didn't make it.

There is no water to witch anymore. Unworkable, the cost of digging, the pumping, all that electricity when I have to tell them two hundred, three hundred, five hundred feet deep. They shake their heads. It isn't magic what I do; I can't conjure it. I can only find it.

And now this news of the bishop. He's coming to close the church. But more than that, he's coming.

This Thursday morning, I have Bob stop the truck just short of his yard. For a new well, I almost always choose a branch from a living tree. A green willow is best, a bit of water still in its body. It has to be green and it has to have give. That's how it finds the stream. And I always start before sunrise.

We set up in the pasture behind the old corral. The slope is better than in front. Higher ground. Less likelihood of ground-water contamination at spring run-off. I begin to pace, like a monk walking his cloister, straight lines back and forth, head bent, arms outstretched, ears open. A choir monk listening for the cantor. My breviary, the divining rod. Nana called it a goddess branch after the Cornish. Palms down, both forks of the wand gripped, one in each hand, I try to feel the water drawing down from the branch, the crook in my hands speaking to the crook in my legs, to the tingling in my feet. The power in me, the power in the wand: intermittent. The feeling of the current is faint in me. Even at my fullest powers, I have to strain to hear it.

I make a widening circle. Not a vibration. A small meadow vole is watching too, worried for its place in the grass. I am careful to watch for and walk around its nest. A hundred paces on I stop and sit. Sometimes that works best for a while. Cross my legs on the earth and empty my mind, just listen for the pace, the rush of water, a faint layer beneath, muffled there, from so high above the surface.

Bob taps me on the shoulder, interrupts my reverie. "Are you sure about that sky?"

I rise again and twenty feet across the pasture, the willow branch jumps in my hands. I mark the spot, have flags ready for the purpose fashioned from old nails and strips of cloth.

I murmur sometimes when I witch. The farmers say I chant. I often close my eyes. There are usually no words, but an intention and a chord that focuses the mind, then a straining to hear the steady hum of the unseen water, the songs calling from beneath. I sway; I hang on and follow where the current takes me.

Yet today, I summon all my powers of concentration, all the spirits I can muster: the dead, the living, saint and animal. I call on them all. "Nana. Papa. Maman." Their names anchoring me; finding an echo in my bones; the electricity in my hands.

The wand wavers. I hold it close to my pelvis, try to stop the shaking in my hands. Then the dream I've had for days breaks in, a harsh dissonance: my young self wakes reaching for breath. Arms crossed over chest, the straitjacket pulled tight behind me. So tight, I cannot move. A young Bishop Leo, a priest then, standing over me; his words stripping me, harsher than any indignity he might have performed. Inside the straitjacket in my dream, my hands won't stop shaking. The rod pulls down hard, starts to shiver; my hands sweat.

"I thirst," I say to no one in particular.

KRISTIAN MUELLER

The white-haired lady is circling the fields like a squirrel, head bent, fast up and down, down and back, around and around. We are waiting for the usual Thursday morning drop-off.

A couple months back, I told the dealer over at the Locke place, "I wanna start a superlab."

"But you're a user."

He's a man in black with intense red at the centre. I focus on the red and ignore the black. Red is strong, cool. The black wigs me out.

"It affects me different than other people."

"Yeah, right." He shook his head.

"Hey, I'm the calmest I ever am when I'm using."

"If the baker eats all the buns, there's none left for the customers."

"I've got a partner. My best friend, Andy, eh. One of us will always be on duty."

He laughed, stepped right into my face. "The more you use it, friend, the more you need it."

I didn't back away. "I can get the ammonia," I said, nodding behind me. "*Anhydrous ammonia,* for nothing." Liquid fertilizer. Tanks of it everywhere you look around here. My old man's, our neighbours'.

His eyes lit up at the Latin. "Okay," he said slowly, eyeing me with new respect. "You've done your research. I'll talk to the boss."

A week later, we had a deal.

Mr. Lechenko, my Chem 20 teacher, would be proud.

I salvaged a nice double sink, a few tables. Bought a couple of coolers and plastic gas cans. Stole the tubing from the science lab at school. The tank, oversized beakers, three-necked flasks. Lots of extras in the cupboards.

Equipment along the wall: goggles, heavy rubber gloves, needle-nosed pliers, three Class D fire extinguishers. Shelving to hold the supplies: cold tablets for the pseudoephedrine — twenty-four-hour Sudafed is the best — Energizer Lithium AA batteries, naphtha, distilled water, rock salt. Ice in the freezer — I found an old fifteen cubic foot in the dump. Still works.

I put down a mattress under one of the tables and crash there if I need to.

I told the Man in Black, the best drop-off is half a mile north, the ditch across the road from Bob Taylor's. He lives alone. No animals. A hobby farmer, city guy. He won't notice. Every Thursday we bring the product and the dealers leave behind all the inputs, except the fertilizer. We make contact the day before on the cell. What's on your shopping list? We have a code for everything. Cold tablets: candy. Batteries: juice. Naphtha: nappies. They pay me a cut of the product plus rights to sell locally. Where else can I make $2,000 plus benefits, cooking for three hours a week? All of it in cold hard cash.

Andy's let me drive his black Trans Am. The morning sky is dark as ink, puffed high with clouds, the thunder coming in quick, every five seconds, then every three, then every two. I am count-ing — a split second later the storm is on top of us. Wind, lightning, but hardly any rain.

She is lit up white like a bulb, rigid at first, then floating. She comes like a ghost across the fields, she comes straight for us. I tell you I saw it straight; I wasn't using.

The old woman keeps coming, through the barbed wire fence, not over but through, like her molecules had come apart and recon-stituted themselves as mist, as mirage. As if she were a cloud floating, yet everything about her is a body.

Next thing I know she's standing right out in front of the car. "Kristian," she calls out.

I don't know how she knows my name.

Andy is there with me. That's how I know it wasn't some weird after-effect of the drugs. He sees her too, but he can't hear her. "Holy Shit!" He's bug-eyed at first.

"Kristian," she keeps calling, inching closer and closer to the windshield, over the hood. "You have killed a living creature in anger."

"No!" I try to plug my ears, put my head down.

Then she shows me not with words but with a picture in my mind: the nosy magpie, when I was building the crack shed, that would hang out on top of the stack, bring his friends, make a racket, beak off at me. Yesterday I had the idea. "Heh, skedaddle, you crazy magpie," I yelled up the skylight at him. "Scram. Beat it. Get lost." Then I opened the valve and let him have it. A shot of ammonia out the vent. He screamed, wheeled screaming, farther and farther away. "Serves you right," I shouted after him.

"Let's go," says Andy.

"What about the deal?"

"Fuck the pickup. They're probably not coming with this storm. Anyways, we can check the ditch later."

Then Andy leans over, lays on the horn. The old lady is standing in front of us again. He's yelling out the window. "Get off the road! Get outta here!"

But she won't budge.

"You're going to have a son, Kristian. Take care of him."

"A son?" How the hell does she know? I'm thinking in my private heart.

"Gun it," says Andy.

"I can't."

"Do it," he shouts at me and shoves my foot down on the gas pedal, the weight of his shoulder against my right side.

And she is under the wheels, her legs, her torso, her raised hands, her head. No thump, no resistance, no weight, just gone.

"There's nothing there!" Andy is yelling. "Who is she?"

I glance in the rear-view mirror. My dad used to say she was an Old Country witch. But back on the road, she looks deader than a doornail. No more light, just a body. I've killed her. I've killed her!

"Dear God." I haven't prayed since I was a little kid. "I'll stay clean. I'll get a job. I'll go back to school." I'm not sure who I'm talking to or what I'm talking about.

Andy punches me in the shoulder then, getting hold of himself, getting the cool back. "Hey, bro. She's gone."

Then I shut up, but I don't stop praying.

JACK RAMSAY

I wake having felt her close, the weight of her hand ruffling my hair, her lips on my earlobe, the way she likes to play after we make love, to keep me awake. But wrenched from me, not unlike the force I've seen when the witcher wand marks a change in energies: water or mineral. Violently. She pulls me up by the hand.

I rub my eyes, glance at the twin curtains sucked out the window, the leaves of the trees showing their backs, trees and shrubs bent low, leaning east. I am alone in my bed. The sun should be rising I tell myself, but the firmament at 6:05 is pitch black. A few seconds later and the foundation seems to explode under and around me. Thunder. And that's when I realize something is wrong.

"Annie!"

I grab my trousers off the chair beside the bed, pull on last night's shirt, my suspenders. Fumble for my cane. Tell myself to calm down. Find the phone on my night table. I'll call Bob; they'll be having coffee. But the answer comes from another direction. Even before I have hobbled over to the window, I have narrowed the location of the siren to the north road. My knees give out. *Go to the hotel.* The hotel? *And wait for me.* The voice comes from somewhere, and I obey. I drag myself to the front door, grab my windbreaker, and the spare set of keys. Right myself, stretch once high over my head. Stumble through the door.

I do not hurry. I know there is no hurrying now. I know as sure as the day. The clouds are apocryphal overhead; the heavens still cracking. One magpie balances on top of the back stop on the ball diamond, fighting to hold her own against the wind. She barks at me softly, lowering her beak and her brow, shifting weight from foot to foot, in time with the wind gusts. I recognize her from the night before. For a few moments, I bow and shuffle into the wind too, thinking this is bereavement: not knowing where to stand or how to walk.

Finally, I let myself in the back door of the hotel. Retire my stick to the boot rack. Follow the hall into the kitchen. Flip to today's date on the at-a-glance wall calendar, by the phone: Thursday, June 8th.

See the note for me by the percolator: "Help yourself. Should be back about nine."

And that is exactly what I do. Pour a cup of coffee and wait.

I am looking out my living room window, my worrying window I call it. Thinking about the secret meeting at the hotel last night to save the Catholic Church from closure. The History Project we're calling it, to buy up the property, or steal what we can if all else fails, out from under the bishop. I'm looking and taking the measure of the sky, the light, a chalky yellow. Thinking about Mike's phone call afterwards, the magpie funeral he witnessed at the schoolyard. Whoever heard of such a thing?

I watch the black SUV skid by on the gravel, givin 'er. Wonder what spooked them this morning? Oh, I know who they are. I have their licence plate. I'm saving it for an opportune time. I see the lightning, see the thunderheads piled high, hear the thunder clap close. The burning smell like cordite through the open window, and beside it, a faint smell like sour gas, something I've been noticing more and more these past weeks when the wind comes up.

That field used to flood every spring. My brothers and I used to take makeshift rafts out on it, old stoneboats. That was before all the sloughs and the creeks were drained. The days before the advice of the district agriculturalist and the farm credit corporation. All those brochures they'd put out: *How to Maximize Your Yields* and *How to Increase Your Arable Land*. Late spring, when the air was rank with spearmint and peppermint, the creek edges lined with it, heading out along the ditches. Those days before progress was king.

I turn back to my breakfast, start opening cupboards, shuffling dishes, find a mug, flip on the kettle switch, dig out a tea bag. Pour dried oats into a bowl, turn on the tap, stir in water, grab an old plate for a cover, open the microwave door, and place the mixture inside. Hit the soup button.

Yes, I am a product of the age too, no matter how much I resist it. Everything's got to be instant these days or the public won't buy it. There's no time for anything else. Still, some things I won't compromise. Eat what you sow, my father used to say. Don't feed your animals anything you wouldn't eat yourself. Oats, same as the cows for breakfast.

That's why I'm here on this earth, so people everywhere can put cereal of some kind in their mouths in the morning and beef on their plates at night. Simple as that. No ground-up pieces of your own kind, organic or not. Protein supplements they call them: a euphemism for cannibalism. The BS in BSE.

I wait for the beep of the microwave, grab a canister, open the lid, and take out a pinch of brown sugar, just the way my mother used to do every morning. The action, like saying Good Morning to her, her canister set. Homemade riveted brass, small designs of a rooster, a hen and chicks etched on each one. There used to be six in the set, now down to three. I miss a feminine presence around here. Bob Taylor's still got his wife's voice on the message machine. Spooks some people, but I understand it. My own wife has been gone for eight years now. Ex-wife, I guess. Not what I signed up for, she said. But is it ever? Set me back a pile, had to re-mortgage the place, then this bloody BSE hit. Our son is graduating high school this year but wants nothing to do with the farm. That pains me.

I take my bowl and my cup of tea over to the worrying window, prop them against the sill. Together they make a small cloud of steam against the pane. I stand there, observe the silence, the closest thing I do to prayer these days, and watch while the sun proceeds red and brilliant on the southeast horizon, not far from the new well where the cattle are lining up already at the trough. I hear another vehicle on the road, this time with a siren flashing, see it barrel down the middle towards Bob Taylor's place. An ambulance. I put my tea down with a thunk, almost knock my porridge off the sill. It's been years since I've seen an emergency vehicle on this road. Not since Hans Mueller's wife took ill.

The lightning is making another jagged scrawl across the sky. The trees bending flat, dancing limbo in the wind. Strange weather. The steers jerk up their heads, step on the toes of their fellows, the thunder and the siren rippling through the herd like a small unnatural eruption.

I know something bad has happened. Nature, whether human or elemental has struck a blow.

VERA PAWLUK

When they bring her in, I've just got on shift. We haven't even had a report yet. Bob Taylor is with the ambulance. She's on a stretcher. The first thing we notice are her clothes hanging by a few shards of fabric on her body and the back of her shirt blown off by force. Her work boots have separated, tops from bottoms. Then we see the markings around her head, neck, and shoulders. "Arborescence," the doctor remarks, "distinctive of lightning strike." A minute later we find the puncture wound at the back of the neck where the lightning has entered her body. Instinctively, I reach down and close her eyelids.

Bob has tried resuscitation, as has the emergency crew all the way in the ambulance, but there was no response. The doctor is puzzled. She must have been leaning forward or crouching. Was she gardening?

Bob sputters, twists his hands, tries to speak, stops. Tries again, flaps his elbows, folds his head to his chest.

Suddenly it dawns on me. "She was witching for water."

The doctor looks up, Bob unfolds himself and nods.

She told me after the meeting last night at the hotel that she was off early today to find a well. She hadn't said for whom.

The doctor wants to know how I knew her. "She was a friend from church," I say quickly.

And I was kind of like a daughter to her, I thought to myself, the shock just starting to register. "She had no family to speak of," I say aloud. And finally the most obvious connection, "We were neighbours."

With that he signs the death certificate. *Cardiac arrest due to lightning strike.* "Better take care of arrangements," he says, watching me closely, glancing at Bob and back to me. "If you need the day … it's still early in here. We'll be able to cover for you." In the entrance-glass afterwards I see my face has turned as white as a doctor's coat.

Bob wants to call the funeral home, but I say, "Listen, Annie left me instructions. She wanted a home laying-out."

His eyes bug out.

"Years ago now," I hesitate. "When she was very sick," I halt again, "and I was looking after her, and she thought she might die, she told me what she wanted."

"If I ever end up in the Emerg," Annie had told me.

"Oh you're far too healthy," I'd said to her. "You're as strong as an ox."

I thought of this now as Bob Taylor stood in front of me looking beside himself.

"Bob. Don't blame yourself." I touch his arm to emphasize the point.

Her voice was low and guttural at the time and weary. "If I drop dead, I want you to take charge of laying me out. I don't want any embalmer, especially any male getting close to my internal organs. Between you and Florence, you'll know what to do. No needles injected, no stitching or cutting or stretching to make me look better than I was in real life. Put me in the ground whole. Understand?"

Annie had never had a doctor or not one that I knew of. And she didn't trust them anymore than she trusted priests, from what I could tell. She didn't trust anyone in the health care professions, she said. But she trusted me because she knew my father and because she knew me since I was a child.

"Sure, Annie," I'd said. "Of course. No embalming. I'll talk to Florence if it comes to that."

"She wanted her women friends," I repeat now, looking up at Bob.

"Okay." Bob squares his shoulders, takes a deep breath. "I can call Florence."

"Maybe Daisy too."

"Okay. I'll call them both."

"See if they can meet us at the hotel in half an hour. Ask Florence to bring some clean clothes. She has a key for Annie's. We can follow in my car.

"And Bob, she knew the dangers of the elements better than any of us. It must have been her time."

He manages to nod; I give him a big hug.

"Give me twenty minutes. I'll start the last offices."

As soon as I've said it, I know I shouldn't have. Bob blanches.

"What I mean," I say, rushing to explain, "I'm going to dress the body for transfer. It's routine. Once you've made the calls, get yourself a coffee." And I wave him through the doors and down the hall to the cafeteria.

I pull the hospital drapes shut, lay down my bundle of towels, cotton batten, and scissors, and stand for a minute in silence. It is something I have witnessed before of the dead, the feeling of the spirit leaving the body. "Dear Annie," I manage, resting my hands on the top of her head. Then slowly I start to cut off scraps of denim and what remains of Annie's plaid shirt. She's always worn such colourful plaids, always overalls, and nothing underneath. Suddenly a fresh rose falls out of one torn pocket. No stem, just the bloom. I pick it up carefully and lay it with her valuables, grab a sponge and water and some antibacterial soap and wash her body quickly as if it were any body and not that of a close friend. There will be time to grieve later, to wash her again and more deliberately among friends. Here for fear of infection and there for the chance to touch her body one last time.

I stuff all the orifices with cotton batting. Wrap the head in towels. Wrap the wrists in gauze then tie them together in front. Leave the silver band that was on her left ring finger. Dress her in a nightgown, the newest and best fit I can find in the linen room. She is thinner than she seemed in real life, bonier than I expect. I fill in the mortuary tag, "Majestic Hotel." Give the address: Railroad and Main. List all the items Bob has found nearby that had escaped her shredded backpack — flags, small hammer, jack knife, water bottle, notebook, wallet, rosary, and rose — place them in a large Ziploc bag and tie the tag to her right big toe.

ANNIE

First thing when we got to his yard, Bob brought me a rose from his garden the colour of sunrise, placed it in my hands. I breathed it in. So many delicate skies. My nana brought roses with her on the boat. Several varieties, clippings from the coast of Cornwall, wild and tame, some from ruined estates, their gardens all that remained. They might have come from Arabia or Persia she liked to say. She kept them fed in a special pot her mother had given her, fitted with a lid of leather, holes poked through to anchor the stems. She poured a bit of her water ration into the pot every day, laced it up tight again afterwards. She treated that pot like a baby, carried it with her wherever she went on board, made sure it got heat and light. The stems grew roots on the crossing. She planted them that spring full of high hopes: damask, gallica, alba, bourbon, and rugosa. What she must have thought that first year in Canada. Cornwall milder yet than London, roses till Christmas. Her winter garden in the western territories, white: a few wild berries, bare bushes, the ground frozen solid. All of the roses perished that first winter but one. A white rugosa still thrives on the old place and blooms gloriously every summer. Even in drought. And then she learned about the shrub roses bred here and the pink wild rose and traded with neighbours who had brought their own gardens with them too, and crossed the pollens and did the grafting herself.

Bob wanted me to witch a well for his late wife's rose project. At first I had pangs of conscience about that. All the farmers trying to grow animals, grow grain, grow food. But then I thought of my nana, how hard she worked to grow the roses in her yard. The cups of dishwater she would feed them at night, the basins of handwashing water. Nothing wasted. They were emblems of beauty; fiery badges of loss, remembrance, what Bob wanted too. So I resolved to go help him find water.

Nana taught me to witch when I was still a child, before I was even in school. She made me aware, casual-like of the forces. She picked up a willow switch and pretended to tell a tale. "A nice young couple," she said. "Just new to the district. Starting out on nothing. He loves her dearly. All the fullness and roundness of her. She has eyes for no one but him. She's going to have a baby. Three months gone already. And they need your help. They've asked you for a well."

She wouldn't wear shoes when she did it. Her skirts flowing around her. Her hair in a bunch on the top of her head. Her eyes closed.

She kept the wormwood and mint and bee balm and heal-all hanging in bundles from her kitchen ceiling, my ceiling now. The local people came to her. She had the hands for curing and for divining. She told me that back in the Old Country the wells were blessed every year, dressed in flowers, sung to, worshipped. That water was gift.

"Think of the Blessed Virgin Mary, the Mother of God," she told me. She kept a shrine to the Virgin, all her roses, the fruit trees in the back of the house, dedicated to her.

Then she said, touching her body where her womb would be: "Listen for the sea."

There comes a moment when you're witching when you know you've found water. Something jolts you awake and pushes you back. The forked branch rises and bangs you in the chest. Something goes out of you. It's the force of life.

It's the same when someone close dies — you can feel it — something brings you up short, knocks the breath out of you. It's like there's a hole in the world and you know a fellow creature has passed. Someone you have loved. Or a birth, the sheer violence of life coming into this world. What Kelsey will be undergoing soon. Witchers feel these things more than others.

KELSEY SANDS

At first it was so fun. We'd go to these bush parties, dance all night, make out. Everything was electric, intense. Like nothing I'd ever felt before. The meth makes me feel like I am this big, wonderful person and my life is a fist of fireworks exploding.

After that, straight is boring. School, home, b-o-r-i-n-g, I tell my mom. I come home in the day time when she's at work. Crash, shower and leave again. I'm never hungry and I feel skinny for the first time in my life. After a while though we quit dancing and we quit making out. We were just out of it all the time. Kristian started to get paranoid.

One morning I woke up sick and puked my guts out and the next, and the next. When I went to the school nurse, she gave me a blue stick to pee on. It came up pink and then a plus sign. We did the test twice. Two days apart.

"Pregnant," she pronounced. "You're pregnant." Her eyebrows caved in. She had this big worried look on her face.

When I told Kristian, he just freaked out.

"Weren't you taking something?"

Like it was all up to me.

"You could have used a condom, but you were too high to put one on, like I asked you."

"I can't support a baby," he says. "I don't have my fucking life together yet and you don't either."

But I don't want to party any more. Something captivates me about this little person growing inside me. Something smaller than me, larger than me. I want to protect it.

I try to talk to my mom. "I'm in real trouble. I'm scared."

Her eyes go right to the place. She can tell from the way I'm holding my belly with my hands, protective-like, and she says, "I've busted my back for you and this is what I get to show for it? Failing at school and knocked up at fifteen?"

My mom cooks at an old folks' home in Victoire. She hates it but it's all she can get with a grade-ten education. She works twelve-hour shifts, four days on, four days off. She makes seventeen bucks an hour.

"I warned you about that Mueller kid. I warned you about the crowd he runs with."

"Mom—"

"I don't want to talk to you right now. Get out of my sight. I wanted—" she hides her face in her hands. I hate it when she cries. "I wanted more for you!"

And I ran into the yard and squirrelled up under one of Miss Annie's lilac bushes.

I used to think it was that easy. You fall in love. You have babies. You set up house. That's what you talk about with your best friends. At noon hours now, I watch the little kids across from the high school in Victoire play fort, play house, play Red Rover. Think how it wasn't long ago that I was that age. How it's all changing.

ANNIE

For decades now, I've avoided the church when Leo Belanger's passed through on bishop duties, made myself scarce.

I don't know how to explain this to Jack, feel illiterate in the language of love. When I open my mouth to begin, all the fear rushes into me: Less-than. Keep-the-secrets, Annie. Temptress-made-invisible. Spooked, I want to say. Ashamed, still. A bottle of whisky, all it would take to obliterate the bishop's young face inside of me, the reproach in his voice. The erasure would be instantaneous. And so I say nothing.

2

MIKE PAWLAK

This here is a canvas of the townsite of Majestic or what's left of it. Used to be a few hundred people living here; the census last year said the population was ninety-eight. It's hard to know the lived-in quarters from the abandoned because they look about the same. Houses with weathered paint and sagging porches. Trailers with missing windows, patched with cellophane, crumbling on their blocks. Fences leaning, stop signs shot through. The whole place has gone literally to the dogs that run loose through the village. Still there's a kind of dignity to it, a tribute to a time when the outlook was more prosperous.

I've always wanted to paint but it's not the kind of thing a grown man says out loud around here. It could be tolerated in a female or an old geezer. Women are prone to flighty ideas and old men to sentiment, but even so, there has never been another painter in Majestic. Not one that I knew about at least. I haven't even told Vera. Only Alex knows and that was by accident.

This painting here is my best friend Alex MacIver's home place three years ago, just before the drought. A barley bumper crop out back. No one knew then what we were on the edge of. See these nice straight barns, all the fine, big cattle, English Poll Hereford-Angus cross. Baldy, we call them. Black with white patches on their face and body. I breed the toughest cows in the country. They can survive any kind of weather. Alex is one of my best customers. He crept up on me early one morning as I was sketching in my truck, scared the living daylights outta me, but he's been my biggest booster ever since. Pushed me to get it all down. Told me his grandmother was a trained artist back in Ontario. He has some of her pencil drawings hanging in his living room.

I set up a work table in the machine shed, near the furnace. Installed a fan, roughed in a new vent. I started last winter — afternoons after all the farm chores were done, I'd slip in there, away from the phone and the cattle.

Vera's a nurse at the hospital in Victoire, working all kinds of shifts. When she asks what I've been up to — Oh, just puttering or cleaning up the shop. Instead I am on the internet, ordering paper, pencils, paint, learning how to mix pigments and to layer paint, how to stretch canvas and make a frame, how to care for the brushes made from pig's bristle and marten tails. Annie Gallagher might suspect: she runs the post office out of the hotel. But she's the kind of person you can count on to keep a secret.

The painting books call my style folk art. That's because there's no perspective. Just by looking, you're right there. That's how it is living here. Just by being, you're in the picture.

See this dark oil, this was one of my first. The old elevator, long torn down. I was still a kid when they quit using it. Not enough traffic to justify the expense. Fire trap, they said. Sold it for salvage. Can't find wood like that anywhere anymore: Douglas fir from the mountains, virgin forest. Twelve-by-twelves and ten-by-tens, some of them solid beams. Can't find construction like that anyhow.

The way planks were fitted together like a puzzle: two-by-tens, two-by-eights, two-by-sixes, and two-by-fours stacked for strength, built to hold tons.

And this painting's of the railway station. Been no train through here in forty years. Solid cedar and it's still standing. Soon they'll be tearing this station down and it will be gone too. People have forgotten where their daily bread comes from. But here's something the city folk will still try to buy — this picture a testament — the nostalgia of country life, the dream of going places and starting fresh.

This was Old Man Brown's house. Eaton's two-storey, thirty by thirty. Came prepackaged on the train eighty-five years ago. Douglas fir and cedar plank let to weather naturally. Sagging in a couple of places but most of it standing as square as the day it was raised. The dovetailing and cross-hatching still in place. A fine house with diamond cut-out windows, Edwardian casements, turn-of-the-century craft. Not much left like that in these parts. The town do-gooders tore it down this spring — part of their beautification project, to make Majestic a more attractive tourist destination. I argued that the only tourists we get ride ATVs through private land or travel the hardtop into town each week to deal in drugs and neither would notice the change.

The dealing happens out on the old Locke place, across the tracks, just out of town. Everyone knows. Hans Mueller's son, Kristian, is mixed up with it. The cars are lined up, the chimney smoking, the door of the trailer open. Kids come by at intervals. Jack Ramsay says they use an electric red and white Christmas candle in the grimy front window, to signal when they're open, like a fish and chip shop. You go inside, they have a menu on the wall, all in code, and they take your order.

Alex told me he used to walk down that road when he couldn't sleep, to try to clear his head, but he doesn't go out walking after dark anymore. One night one of those young punks almost ran him off the road, threatened him with a baseball bat. They burned rubber in circles around him, laughing like hyenas, before gunning it to the highway. The RCMP say they're watching. Maybe by satellite. We don't see them here unless we phone them. GRCS, gravel road cops.

This oil painting is of the school the way it used to be. Tall glass windows, each pane a dozen squares of glass. I can remember when I sat and looked out those windows: watched storms; watched the magpies, jays, and hawks, the wind move the grass; watched gophers stand in their holes out on the ball diamond, the snow melt and water run through the streets of town in early spring. By the time I got to grade six, I had learned all I needed to of weather systems and aerodynamics, of prey-predator relationships and the properties of water. But now they have most of the windows closed in, the rooms lit with fluorescent tubes, all to keep out distractions.

This painting is of the Majestic hotel. It's been here for a good seventy years. Annie's father built it when he got out of the brick business in 1931, with the piles of discards he had on the old kiln site. Finished the fir doors himself, the door jambs and the wainscoting up the staircases inside. It proved a lucrative business in the thirties, people came from all around to drown their sorrows. When Annie took over the hotel in the sixties, she added the mail counter, mailboxes, and the coffee nook — just a table in the lobby. It's probably the most beautiful building we've got in Majestic. The church is solid construction and the stained glass is nice, but the red klinker bricks of the hotel are hard to beat.

This painting is of the old brickyard — half of it reclaimed by the forest, poplar and wild rose growing through crooked piles of klinker bricks. The rough ovens are collapsed, but you can still see where they set the green bricks into the fire, bucked up the archways, shoved in the cord wood or coal. Technically this land still belongs to Annie, but she has no desire to resurrect it. I approached her once about fixing it up, making it into a little outdoor museum for the school kids, interpretive signs, walking paths, a footbridge over the old creek bed. But Annie said she preferred to let it go back to itself, the original footbridge dynamited in the thirties already.

This one here I call the Table of Truth — the coffee circle at the post office inside the Majestic hotel. You can see us gathered near the mailboxes. Everyone shows up for the mail: the old, the middle-aged, and the eagers (for eager beavers). There's always one or two new-to-towners, cottagers or acreage dwellers wanting to live the country life. Most of the young farmers just walk right by when they see us with our mugs of coffee and our slow stories. "Got work to do," they quip. Some you can entice to talk about the weather, their crops — for a quick minute — and then they take their leave.

Their time will come. Comes quick enough if you're in farming: the markets drop; hailstones rain from the sky, pulverize young shoots; snow downs a crop. You can't make the payment on your loan. You have to take that first town job. The wife leaves you. Everyone's got his breaking point.

I can't really do it justice, the feeling at the Table of Truth or the people's faces on such a small canvas, but I've given each one something that marks them as separate.

See how Jack Ramsay wears a fedora, fawn in colour. The hat is unusual in these parts, but it fits his personality. He's a geologist, born here, moved away, and moved back. A man of many worlds, a man of intellect. He's at the age where he needs a cane, but he still walks pretty much everywhere.

That's Buster Goodchild there with his pipe. He doesn't smoke it anymore, but he still likes to chew on the old thing. Says it keeps his hands busy. Buster's an old cowboy — Stetson, leather jacket — right down to the boots. Getting up in years. This bovine spongiform encephalopathy, BSE thing has hit all of us hard, but especially Buster. A surplus of livestock but no markets. The border, closed. When this does get sorted, ten years or never, it'll be too late for him to make up the loss.

In this picture, all eyes are on the "new guy" in the circle. Bob Taylor's lived here eighteen years, but he's still considered new in town. It's different than being born here, going through school together, marrying, birthing, taking over your people's land. Scientists can read the composition of a skeleton like the rings of a tree. The minerals of a place lodge in your bones. It takes generations to belong.

You can't tell from the painting, but Bob's a tall, lanky fellow. Wears black horn-rimmed eye glasses, early fifties. Black hair combed to the side, a few strands of grey. Construction contractor. Moved here with his wife. Both commuted to work in the city for years. They were going to retire on that quarter section too, then she got ovarian cancer last year. Died. Just like that.

They're debating land use — townies versus farmers. Hobby farmers versus the real thing. Acreage owners versus everyone else. The county plans to subdivide quarter sections, parcel them up into forty acre lots and sell them to the townies.

Land prices will skyrocket. Some don't like the added cost of services, schools, the new paved roads that will be built, the traffic, the taxes that will have to rise. And all for what? Some will drive their kids to city schools anyways. The townies will be in a hurry all the time, late for work. It'll be dangerous to move machinery along the roads.

In this picture, everyone's watching Bob. He's taken the family farmer's side, though he rents most of his quarter section to Alex

MacIver. "What about food production?" he's saying. Some of the older ones would like the option of selling off pieces at a time, sort of like money in the bank or old age security of which there is none in modern-day farming. Though they won't say so out loud, he's got their attention. They wish they could be as idealistic. But then he's relieved of all responsibility for practicality with his wife's untimely passing and that rose memorial he's got in mind.

And this one, I just finished. It's St. Joseph's, built in 1915, on a hill that runs along the west side of town. I'd been waiting on the church, I thought it might be bad luck to paint it before the For Sale sign went up. As if recording it for posterity might make the sale a certainty and jinx the scheme that's afoot.

Now that the closing is immanent, I've been making quick sketches, mornings before the post office opens, the post office my only excuse to get into town most days. How to depict a place so ordinary that means so much? I'll stop the truck behind the hotel or down the hill to the north, trying different angles.

It's plain enough, white stucco with bits of glass stuck in the mortar. The foundation, though, is a thing of beauty. Built like a European fortress, five feet thick, quartz and granite erratics mixed with cement. Rocks from the fields — that is what holds it up. These fields, this earth, these farmers. A squared bell tower and brass bell but no steeple. The panes of stained glass, simple solid colours, letting the light and glass speak for itself. Douglas fir frame and siding. Local birch for the flooring.

It's hard to show what I see. All the generations that have worshiped here. All the marrying and burying that has taken place. As the highest point of land, it's the first building in town to enjoy the sunrise, morning light coming through the sanctuary, during Sunday Mass. The gathering place it's become: parents dropping their little ones off to daycare every morning or the crowds that come out to our Friday night concerts: bluegrass, folk, and country. The annual fall supper. It's a place of animation.

And this is my latest sketch. From last night after the meeting at the hotel, a scene as I was driving home, in the poplars behind the playground at the school. Every branch of every living tree and the dead ones too, lined with birds, shoulder to shoulder. Must have been a hundred magpies calling at the tops of their lungs, croaking in an unrelenting lament, you'd think someone had died. Some were wheeling overhead and taking turns touching down as if to pay their last respects. I stopped the truck, took out my binoculars, and spotted one of their own lying on its back on the ground, legs in the air, the mourners looking down on their fallen fellow. Equal to any such show of feeling in humans. Was it felled by another bird, a hawk or a merlin? Was it school children playing a prank? I searched for a scrap of paper in the glove compartment, drafted quickly their half-leafy, half-stark silhouettes, and called it Magpie Funeral.

VERA

Almost every time I go into the shed to find a hammer, get an extension cord or a screw driver, I can smell the fumes. The other day, I wandered to the back corner, where I found a black-bound journal on top of a table next to the computer Mike uses to do the farm accounting. I opened it. It held sketches of the home quarter, of Majestic and its people. Most in black and white, some in the faintest wash of colours, some with the colours written in, prototypes for a painting. I set it back where I'd found it.

At first I was amazed. My husband, the painter! But then I shouldn't have been. When I thought about it, I've always known how observant he is of people and of the land. Always walking around with an eye wide open to the world.

And there's no need to say anything. Each of us has our need for an inner life, something private from the other. I hadn't known I'd married an artist. Better than gambling or alcohol or another woman.

Farming is tough. I get a farmer at Emerg every couple of weeks complaining of chest pains, back pains, headaches, ashen in the face, hyperventilating. I do the initial intake before the doctor sees them:

Have you been under any stress lately?

How much alcohol have you consumed this week?

Have you had any recent losses?

How well are you sleeping?

They can barely talk.

We run them through the tests, put them on the treadmill, shoot them up with adrenaline. We order CT scans on their chests, send them to the city to get MRIs on their heads. Their vitals come back normal. Much of it is worry or just plain working too hard. Long days, short anxious sleeps. All day the body going. No help to be got. Everyone's working double-time between home place and town, farm chores and second job, just to keep up.

If the problem persists, the doctor prescribes sleeping pills or antidepressants. The doctors here hand those out like candy. The worst cases get a prescription for Ativan. A tiny pill the shape of a house, square with a peaked roof. It's so innocuous, it's dangerous. Relief is instant, euphoric. The doctor doesn't explain, only "When you feel an anxious spell coming on, take this." Warns them not to operate any heavy equipment. When they run out, they invariably come back for more.

Alex MacIver was our most recent visitor. Alex is a cow and calf man. We have a lot of that around here. He presents every few months with chest pains. Calving season is the worst, February and

March, up all times of the night, in all weathers. Out in the pasture looking for birthing cows, pulling calves, warming them up in the barn if it's a cold night. Hundreds of cows too many for one man. Always behind with seeding and swathing and raking. Always last in the field with the combine.

"When was the last time you had a good night's sleep?" the doctor asks him. He doesn't remember. There's nothing wrong with him, yet. Nothing that three square meals a day, rest, and some good hired help won't mend. Calving season is pretty much over. On the way out the door, I help him with his coat. They'll let me do that when I've got my uniform on.

"Get the rest of the crop in," I say. "And sell a few head of those cattle, even at a loss. You'll feel better."

He clamps the baseball cap firmly forward on his head, barely meets my gaze, and walks out the automatic doors. He can't afford my medicine.

3

FATHER PAT COLLINS

When I came here three years ago, that hotel, just down the hill
from the church and the rectory, was staring at me every morning,
and me just out of treatment and trying to stay sober. That hotel is
one thing I won't miss about this place. One of my parishioners —
if you can call Annie that — she attends Mass but never joins in
anything — is the proprietor. Then there's Daisy who chides me for
not telling her when there's been a small unravelling in the seam
or brocade of the ancient vestments. All so that she can mend them.
They've been ratty for years. Checks them now after every mass. She
runs some kind of kitchen linen business from home. And there's
Florence, the crazy pro-lifer who continually asks me to include a
prayer for the unborn in the petitions at mass.

"The unborn aren't the only ones suffering injustice!" I snap at
her one Sunday. "Perhaps they have it better than the born."

She is scandalized. Claps her hand over her mouth, exits stage
right. Leaves me alone for weeks. Until the bishop calls and makes
me apologize.

Nor will I miss Sunday worship or what passes for worship,

their dogged faces looking back at me every week, begging for a word of hope. The lot of them, a knarled body worn down by loss after loss. The same hymns week after week: *Holy God We Praise Thy Name; Holy, Holy, Holy; Ave Maria; Peace Is Flowing Like a River;* and *O Sanctissima.* No one else seems to mind. When I ask Daisy, she says Thelma Cummins only knows six pieces outside of Christmas carols and that I should be glad she knows that, owing to the fact that piano lessons weren't cheap and organ even more scarce and no one to teach either one now in sixty miles. So we have to make the best of it. Mrs. Graves, the original grade one teacher, taught Mrs. Cummins everything she knew — the notes on the right hand and the chords on the left. Thelma taught herself how to use the organ pedals before she married Tom Cummins. Six kids (and the church's teaching on birth control to blame for that, she is sure to mention) doesn't afford her any more leisure. She's milked the cows and took suppers out to the field for prin'near forty years of an evening (Daisy's words), spring seeding or fall combining, and can't be faulted if she doesn't have time to come to town to prac- tice and learn new material, even as a grandmother. Besides she has arthritis in the wrists now.

In the three years I've been here, I've managed to teach them two new hymns, *a cappella* — which I had to patiently explain is Italian for "without accompaniment" — and I only managed the former because both tunes are in Latin and a couple of the old ladies remembered them from their childhood. *Agnus Dei* and *Dona Nobis Pacem* as a round. That's about as cosmopolitan as it gets in Majestic.

I don't say it to any of them, it's not my place, but the way things are going with the drought and the feed costs and the low prices they get for their beef, pork, and grain, most of them will be out of business in ten years. The smart kids leave. The rest get stuck with the family debt. Big farming multinationals will move in here, take up the best of the land. Developers will sell off what remains as acreages to folks from the city. There won't be anything left of Majestic as we've known it. There won't be anybody left to go to church. Better that we prepare the people for the changes. The church will be the least of their worries. That's what I tell the bishop.

I took this posting on the understanding that it wouldn't be more than two years. That we had to face the demographics and that the bishop would do the right thing and close it. The sociologists, even the evangelicals, know we have to concentrate our efforts on the larger population centres, and get the most out of our limited resources, that being priests. Well, now that day is here.

"I know those people, Pat. Good people. Salt of the earth!" the bishop kept protesting. It took a lot of argument to keep him from reneging. It took the force of reality to argue him out of sentiment, to show him he would not be doing anyone any favours. A Sunday afternoon tour of the district and town, what's left of it, an inspection of the church, and a subtle but pointed request for financial assistance for repairs. He had to come around.

I don't even know why the diocese is bothering to try and sell. It's not worth anything. Plain country church. The best feature is its foundation. In my opinion, I told the bishop, we should just deconsecrate the thing and leave. Say the final prayers, say goodbye to the structure, give thanks for the years. Board up the windows, take out the glass, and take down all the religious objects. The only things of value, and even that, marginal.

"Now I know it's been a hard slog for you out there all on your own, Pat, and don't think I don't appreciate it. I spent most of my priestly ministry in the rural areas. But we can't do that. It's a symbol, after all, of the body of Christ. We cannot just abandon the bride. We must make provisions."

During Easter, the bishop came out to announce they were selling. First time he'd shown his face in years. No other reason. They haven't been confirming the little ones here for a long time. He got up there in all his robes, his staff, his funny gold hat. They even dragged out a special chair for His Grace from up in the choir loft. I suppose so he could set his big bottom on it. He stands up there and tells the people "We're" selling the church, in that royal We way, the diocese is selling. "We've had our consultation." We the people. Consultation they called it, but the decision was already made. "Go home," the suit ties and the clerical collars said like they have for forty years, "and pray for vocations."

One evening in late March, the faithful who have been going for years, those baptized and lived their whole lives here, got up one by one and presented their case — while three suited-up administrators sat behind a table just below the altar, at the top of the aisle, and watched their Rolex watches. Parishioners were limited to five minutes. The parish council chair was given ten. Still the presentations took two hours.

The panel's projector wouldn't work. So Father Pat dragged out an old flipchart that was wedged in one of the cupboards at the back, and we waited while the panellists drew their crooked charts and tables on that. Money and attendance. Shift in population. A shortage of priests.

"A shortage of female intelligence," Annie muttered behind me in her characteristic clever way. But I could tell from her tone that it was an effort for her to be there.

"Miss Annie!" Kelsey protested beside her. But she couldn't stop giggling. She's been living with Annie these past months ever since she told her mother that she was pregnant. It is good to hear her laugh. Thought she'd forgotten how.

"*You're* a priest in the making aren't you?" Annie said to Kelsey matter-of-fact-like.

I concurred, "An altar server."

Kelsey's face got serious then.

Of course she is. Everyone knows it's how priests have been recruited for centuries. First an altar server, then for some, a chosen few who hear the call, priesthood.

About six weeks before, Kelsey had asked to come to church with Annie and when she saw the older ladies on the altar and then the occasional boy, she said, "Hey, I could do that."

"So you could," Annie had said. "So you could."

The only reason Annie had agreed to attend the panel was to support the rest of us. "You know I've never been a speechmaking person," she'd said to us when we first asked her. At the time, I couldn't help but notice a slim shadow of fear flit across her face.

When it was my turn to speak, I stood up and looked them all in the eye. I pointed to the stained glass windows. "Those were twenty years of bake sales. Each one bought and paid for one at a time. Those vestments you wear on Sundays, Father Pat—"

He shifted in his chair when I said that. He never liked drawing attention to himself. But here he was on the hot seat.

"All that gold edging, that was our mothers' work. All their pin money went for thread. What eggs they sold in town, the sacrifice of sweets during Lent, the sacrifice of a new dress, a new hat, the sacrifice of sweet things for a lifetime. Their children without shoes in summer. Made do with skin leggings in winter. Just so's they could set aside to buy the best silk thread for your robes.

"This church is going on ninety years old. Our fathers trowelled the plaster, hammered the beams and laid floor, then carpet, then floor again. Insulated. Lowered the ceiling, raised the ceiling. Repainted and repainted how many times?"

All Father Pat said was, "Why can't you go up the road to Victoire?"

The land is better at Victoire, the farmers richer; the land around Majestic, with our poor grey soils, is boreal country. We are a plainer people, without ecclesiastical ambitions of any kind.

"We are not the same people as Victoire," I said out loud.

He did not follow my meaning in the least. "The church is the people, not the place."

"Don't you see Father," said Vera, rising from her seat, "we are the church in this place!"

VERA

I was ready, my cue cards dog-eared by the time the night arrived. But the consultations were a formality. The bishop didn't attend. He said he wanted an objective opinion from a team of lay experts: one was a consultant from a prominent marketing agency in the city, one a real estate broker, and the other a banker. The bishop said he wanted to remain neutral.

We presented the facts. An increase in attendance, an increase in programming, including a children's program. A service every Sunday, most of them lay-led. Attendance up fifty percent in the past three years. Taxes paid up. A well-maintained facility — a new furnace last year, new casements for the windows — a successful fundraising drive. Even non-Catholics gave. They consider St. Joseph's a historical and community resource.

"But what about the roof?" The banker looked up from his papers, took off his gold-rimmed readers.

"We do need a new roof," I admitted. "We do need help for that."

The suit continued. "These figures are hardly representative, might be statistically misleading when you only have a congregation of one hundred and fifty people and not likely to grow much more. Demographic projections for this area look grim. You'll probably be seeing the last of your catechism classes with this mini-baby boom in the province."

"We've studied the demographics too," I assured him. "We know the population from farming is shrinking but depending on what the county does, the population from acreage dwellers and commuters could sky rocket. Eighty-five percent of new membership this year were former urbanites moved to the country."

The real estate man unbuttoned his sports jacket, looked up. "But none of this addresses the question of ministry."

"We share Father Pat with four other communities. We've sponsored three people from our parish to the diocesan leadership training program. One of them has gone on to study theology. They take turns serving our parish on Sundays when the priest can't attend, giving the sermon and passing out communion. One organizes a special visitation ministry, all volunteers, for the sick and the shut-in."

I saw the marketer bend his head, his eyes focused, his hands disappeared below the table, his elbows moving. Checking his mobile.

I may not have an MBA, but I know this community needs a place to dream itself and if the church in our time won't be the place, then the church of the future will. But there's another question here, one that they refuse to acknowledge but is happening in spite of all their best planning. The church of the future is going to have a lot more women in leadership roles, and I'm going to do whatever I can to make it so.

"Two more lay leaders are in formation and will be able to lead services in a couple of years. We feel we are well positioned for the future. Our finances are in excellent shape. We send money to the diocese every year."

The one with wire reading glasses glanced at the budget sheet, cleared his throat. "A modest donation for a budget in the millions."

For this meeting, Father Pat had opened the parish books to them.

"With respect, Sirs, five thousand dollars is not a small donation for a parish of one hundred and fifty people.

"We host an annual turkey supper that draws more than six hundred people from the area. We host a dance every May Day in honour of Mary and draw that many people easily. That is how we paid for the new furnace last year. We host a joint graveyard clean-up day with the United Church once a year that brings people in from all denominations.

"Last but not least, our finished basement is used as a daycare during the week. School plays are mounted in our sanctuary for the entire community. A local folk club rents our space for a series of concerts every winter. What we gain in rent, we put back into maintenance."

I sat down, my legs still shaking, an ache in the small of my back. Behind me the crowd of two hundred, residents from all around, stood to clap.

At break I heard the marketing kingpin lecturing the other administrators. The cell phone in his hand, doubling as his pointer. "This is the age of big box stores and big box churches. Majestic will never amount to much either economically or socially. All these small churches north of the capital are a problem. No major industry in this area. Small time oil and gas. The growth is going south or further north.

"The people already commute to jobs. They commute for groceries, for dentists, for doctors. It's already an expected part of country living. Why would worship be any different? It's for the common good. And if all else fails you can always remind them that loyal Catholics obey the chain of command."

He caught me watching at that moment. Caught himself, faltered, tried to turn away. I just stared.

FATHER PAT

When I got out of the seminary, I thought I had a clear idea about my future, who I was, and what I could contribute. I'm the priest: the leader, the confidant, the mediator. I thought people would come to me, ask my opinion, even defer to me once in a while. When I got to Majestic, I waited for someone other than the parish council chair to invite me for supper.

After a snowstorm, out shovelling, one of the old guys, Jack, came to help me with my driveway and asked how I was settling in.

I took a chance. "The people," I said, "don't seem very friendly."

He stared at me a minute. "You're not going to like this," he said finally. "But you've got to go to them, Father. Come down to their level. I know you're not a drinking man," he motioned to the hotel, "but if you wait for them to invite you, you're going to wait till the cows come home."

Some of the old guys in the meetings say you get over the craving, you get stronger, so you can be with people who drink, even people who get drunk and not let it bother you. It's true I can drink the consecrated wine every week and I don't feel tempted. But nowhere else, yet.

I press my own cassocks. Do my own laundry. Make sure to shine my shoes every night. I have an old vehicle. A Chev Suburban. I do all my own maintenance. I have the same three television channels as everyone else. I could have got cable, but most here don't.

The only person I might see for days on end is the housekeeper, Rita Chambers. She always looks surprised to see me at home in the middle of the day. When they told me about the housekeeper, I almost dismissed her. I can cook; I can clean. I can take care of myself. Oh, they said as if they knew I'd be lonely, you're going to need her. Now she's often the only person I see all week.

If they only knew what I need or why I'm here. I wonder what they'd say. I had an affair with the director of religious education. A man, not a woman. I have never known how to reconcile it, this attraction I have for men. Wanting to confide in them, needing to be noticed by them, to lie with them. I thought I could escape into prayer, into service. Into celibacy.

We both had to leave the parish. He to another diocese, me to Majestic. It was a scandal, hushed up, like it never happened. As soon as they could, people forgot about it, went on with their business. "We don't have priests like that." That's the thing about Catholics, they don't want to believe it even when it's right in their faces.

I was sent off to rehab for my drinking. The reason, the bishop was sure, why I got involved with my own sex. I didn't know what I was doing.

Even if I had been so inclined, Rita is plain Rita. I think they do that on purpose. Make sure they pick the least likely to pose an obstacle. The most interesting thing she gets up to is watching old episodes of *Star Trek* and attending scrapbooking conventions. She tells me that's her ambition for Majestic. To get a scrapbooking show here one of these years. Like everyone else, she's a one-of-a-kind, but she's not a temptation.

"Bishop," I said, "the main social outing here is the pub. If you want me to stay out of trouble, you're going to have to get me out of here." That was what made him act finally. He had no one to put in my place.

4

ANNIE

Across the road, in the schoolyard, the children dance rhymes. *Ring around the rosie. Pocket full of posies.* They'll play like that for hours if they can. How they skip and sing. They know what's coming: *we all fall down!* They laugh about it.

Three blind mice, three blind mice. See how they run, see how they run.

Maman did not want to be a farmer's wife. She married a man in uniform. The son of a blacksmith with ambitions for industry. Bricks. Nana said my maman wanted a town house and a proper espaliered garden. My father said she wanted a place safe from war. A place far from La Grande Guerre. She had to settle for a two-room shanty of spruce two-by-fours, with curtains for dividers instead of walls, in the outliers of the Canadian West, living next door to a kiln that spilled black smoke seven days and seven nights at a stretch.

The children's voices haunt like a heat mirage on the horizon.

Here we go around the mulberry bush, the mulberry bush, the mulberry bush.

Ah, here's where the preparation begins.

This is the way we wash our clothes.

Yes, so it is. In a way, they're right. The scrubbing, the ironing, the laying out.

On a cold and frosty morning.

Getting their hands ready, they are.

Oats, beans and barley grow. Oats, beans and barley grow. Do you or I or anyone know? How oats and beans and barley grow?

My maman used to grow the fattest fève beans. Nobody knew how she did it. Broad beans in this godforsaken country. Started them as soon as the sun returned to the eastern sky, soaked them a day at most. Placed them beside the small south-facing window in layers. My father built shelves for them. Outside she found the ground with the best soil. She'd string thick cotton sheets overhead to shield the beans from the midday sun. Stake them. Harvest them early in July before the worst of the heat, before the humidity and the pests overtook them. But what was the mechanism, the trigger that made them shuck off their coats and spend all their energies on one green shoot? I asked her once when I was very small. *Je ne sais pas, ma petite.*

It's bound to catch up to you, not knowing how life works. Thinking you can master it. Were it as simple as sowing the seed and clapping. As simple as waiting.

JACK

When I hear the ambulance outside the hotel, I grab my cane, limp my way to the front door, throw it open. The attendants look startled. Bob and Florence are surprised to see me. Vera and Daisy, I think they always knew. "Help me!" I start to head back inside. "The Table of Truth!" I try again, sliding the sugar, the salt and pepper shakers, and the napkin dispenser to the end, removing them one by one to the counter in front of the postal wicket. Bob immediately understands and rushes ahead of the paramedics. Together the three of them turn the table on its side and wedge it carefully through the second door into the main part of the hotel. The women stay with Annie's body. Only when the table is righted again and the attendants have returned to their charge, do I point. "There," I command. "Put her there." And they do.

Vera comes to me and gives me a big hug. "Oh, Jack, I'm so, so sorry." I let my cane topple to the floor. My whole body is shaking. I know if I try to say anything, the tears will come.

Bob is upset too. "She was witch—" But he can't finish.

Vera is the one who tells the others, tells Bob, "Let's give them some time alone. To say goodbye." The women unzip the body bag, gently move her onto the table, her head and body wound in gauze and white linens. Without even seeing her face or the tips of her fingers, I know her presence. And now, Annie Gallagher, whether you wanted it or not, we're known in the public eye.

Last night we stood, an awkward couple, a little apart at the end of the evening; the meeting at the hotel done and put to bed. Me balancing on my one good leg and a little on you. It was our one shared ritual: watching the sun go down at the end of each day at the back of your house.

I said, as I always do, "You are an extraordinary woman, Annie Gallagher," and squeezed your hand, what I do instead of a kiss. All you would allow me in public, even the near-deserted public of Majestic. You would say you're old-fashioned, but I knew there was more to it than that. You were afraid that people would talk, make assumptions about your character. And people do talk. There's no controlling that fact. You had to witch a well in the morning and were leaving early. I tipped my hat, then stood outside your back gate, bent over my cane, waiting to hear the lock click before turning to go, wanting to enjoy the last of the light before ambling into the alley.

Our relationship was always like that. Sometimes close, sometimes distant, the choice inexplicable from one day to the next, even after all these years. You were troubled and folded in on yourself. I knew your love in our touch, but I wished you could trust me with anything. "Anything, Annie," I find myself muttering now. But I learned not to force you.

As it was, I knew the bishop's coming was what was bothering you. I'd heard the stories, so many versions of events. We were a few years apart in grades. What was not in dispute: the police car parked out front of the family home, your disappearance from school, and your return seven years later as a fiercely beautiful young woman. Hurt in some way we could not see but could sense, like the sealed wound in a wild animal. There was no mistaking it.

Last night, back out on the street, on my way home, that's when I saw the magpies, piercing the air with caw after caw after caw. I saw the dead one and I saw the mate, preening the fallen bird's feathers, pecking so softly at his neck. A sob rose in my throat, wanting the fallen bird to stand too. Shivering with sudden cold, shook to my bones, I struck the earth with my cane. I almost defied you, Annie Gallagher, so frightened I was for us. I almost hobbled back to hold you through the darkness, no matter the talk, no matter your fears. I hold you now.

FLORENCE

"All right," I told Bob on the phone, "I know how to prepare the body." When I was a child, undertakers were a city invention. "As long as we have help to move her inside."

Yet all I can think about are the magpies congregated in the schoolyard last night. An old rhyme from childhood comes to mind: *one for sorrow, two for mirth, three for a wedding, four for birth, five for rich, six for poor, seven for a witch, eight for heaven.* We used to chant on the hopscotch court; we used to try to predict: Would it be sorrow? Would it be marriage? Birth? Never for me. Would it be death? We tried to hop quickly over the unlucky squares, land on the lucky ones.

My grandmother used to say, "We were all birds once. When they start to grieve, our sorrow won't be far behind. They're harbingers." They know things. Like when a storm is on the wind, the length and advance of seasons, and when someone's died.

After I was done my dishes, had swept the kitchen floor, and put out the trash, I found my spade and an old towel on the porch and went out to bury the unfortunate creature.

The bird was on his back, head straight, no blood or sign of attack. Did he die of natural causes? Then I noticed the eye swollen shut. What on earth?

That's when I saw the thunderheads gathering again as they had the last night and the night before and the night before that. But nary a drop of water. And I felt the full weight of my eighty-one years of existence. As I do now.

"Yes," I said to Bob over the phone again, "I know how to prepare the body."

I let myself into Annie's house, find food for the cats, and change their water. Fetch the box of burial clothes she had shown me once, on the top shelf of the front hall closet. Get to the hotel just as Bob and Vera and the ambulance arrive with her body.

Jack opens the front door for us. He looks weary, trembling. I am shocked at first. Well, I knew they were close. There were rumours. I knew it was their routine to meet for coffee before the hotel opened. Jack helped her sometimes at the post office. They were often seen together.

But he seems to know; he seems to know and is waiting. Bob tries to speak but starts to weep. Vera rushes ahead to meet him. "She's gone, Jack. She died instantly." He lets out a great howl and pounds his breast when he sees the body bag on the stretcher, the attendants hanging back. He can't breathe at first and collapses. When he finds his voice again, he asks, could we allow him a few minutes with Annie, even with her all wrapped up from the hospital? We find him a chair, set him on it, remove the body bag, and leave the two of them alone. The four of us drink out of the pot of coffee still hot in the kitchen, welcome the bitter taste. We give him a good thirty minutes.

Then, "We have to," Vera, explains to him, "we are sorry, but we have to prepare the body now." He has been crying. We can see that. Vera sends Bob home with him and tells him to come back later in the day, when we are done.

"Yes, yes." Jack nods quickly.

He fixes his eye on the mummy-wrapped body one more time, takes hold of the cane that Bob has retrieved for him, presses his hat to his head, and lets himself be led out the front door.

DAISY

The dead bruise easier than the living, that's what I'm told. The attendants wheel her in on a stretcher and place her carefully on the ancient plank table we have set out in the middle of the public house for the purpose, the table that usually sits in the foyer across from the mail wicket and has a coffee pot on it. Florence says it's the one piece of furniture still surviving from when Annie's father's people came across the ocean. "The Table of Truth" the men call it. After Jack, Bob, and the attendants leave, Florence tells us about the magpies in the schoolyard last night. "For land's sakes!" I can't help the outburst. Then we stand quietly for a moment, the three of us, to pay our respects. Florence makes the sign of the cross.

First, we unwrap the face. Florence and I stand back. Annie is staring at us.

"That's odd," Vera says. "I closed her eyes at the hospital."

Florence reaches over to close them again, but Vera is nervous. "Careful."

Florence steps forward, tries again.

"No, they won't stay. It's best not to force them. They'll bruise and swell and look even worse."

"What about coins?" I ask foolishly, thinking of movies I've seen, pictures of mummies in National Geographic.

"I don't know," Florence says. "She never cared too much for money."

"It would be forcing the skin now," Vera says. "If they don't go naturally, there's nothing we can do."

So we begin to undrape the body, neck first. I've never done this sort of thing before. My hands are all sixes and sevens. Like when I'm learning a new stitch or a new pattern at the shop. And death is certainly a new stitch for me.

When we examine her closely, we see the etchings in the shape of grand trees and ferns branching all along her neck, down her throat, around her shoulders and up her scalp.

I can't help but gasp. "It looks like jewelry," I say and can't stop talking. "I think we should leave some of it showing, at least what we would normally show I mean." I am pleased by this unexpected show of beauty in death. I had expected ugly red gouges or black smears on her skin. My mind takes fanciful flights, thinking how well this might look on a tea towel or a T-shirt. That's when I first get the idea of a memorial of some kind.

"It's like the most beautiful tattoo I've ever seen." I am babbling nonsense I know.

"No," Vera says, "I mean, yes." She shakes her head. "But it's from the lightning."

Florence steps back, stands with her hips apart, flexes her wrists as she sometimes does when she's excited, articulates both palms outward and upward, as if she regularly juggles in her sleep and this were an unconscious vestige of it in waking hours. "Annie's love of living things. The trees, the plants." She clasps her animated hands together. "It's right!"

She's restraining herself. She wants to call it miraculous, I can tell. For once, I do too.

"It is fitting," Vera admits.

We reason that Annie would have wanted the marks to stay. It's just the way she was. No varnish in her life, and she wouldn't want it in her death either.

I find carbolic soap in the hotel kitchen cupboard. Vera brings us each basins with lukewarm water, fresh sponges and washing cloths. We unbind her wrists and hands. Florence locates a few pillows in the hotel stores, places a smaller one under Annie's chin and two more under each elbow to keep the hands crossed.

We look at where the lightning has punctured the flesh, first at the back of the neck and then the palms of the hands and the bottoms of the feet where the current has exited.

Vera warns us we'll see burn marks.

"Like the stigmata," Florence says.

"That's because she was in a crouching position when she was hit," Vera says calmly, "and she always witched with her palms down."

We start off washing her together, the face, the neck, the shoulders, the collarbone, the torso, the small of her waist — all down one side. At first we work in silence. She moves a little while we work, the legs twitch, the feet too, the muscles, the way it is with the dead, according to Florence. Florence is working on Annie's belly when she puts her sponge down and suddenly starts to give orders.

"This isn't the right way to go about this," she says, upset. "Daisy, get us some drying towels from the hotel stores. Vera, find some shampoo. I'll wash. One of you dry. The other, work on her joints."

She is the elder among us, so of course we bow to her wishes.

FLORENCE

What stops me are the scars on the front of her belly. Whiter against white in death. Was it a baby? A caesarian section? Not long enough. Appendicitis? Wrong place. I rinse my sponge, and then I feel her presence in the water. I look up: the others haven't noticed. I feign bossiness, excitable nerves, something I'm known for, and send the two of them off on errands. I turn back to the body and keep washing. Every time I dip the sponge, I ask her a question.

"Do you remember the time I came to your grandmother's house?"

"I was staying over that weekend." Annie's voice is whispery, trembling-like.

"You remember what happened?"

"I remember your screams. But women often came to scream and then they left happy."

"Do you remember how long it took?"

"It seemed all night to me."

"All night and all day."

"Your grandmother gave me an herb. No scissors or knitting needles. No pointy sticks. Just tea and she prayed to the Virgin. God forgive me. She knew I could not have that baby."

"I didn't know how to comfort you."

"You fed me chicken soup."

"You wouldn't eat at first. You wouldn't take anything."

"Till your grandmother told me she could not abide two deaths." I bend my head, bring my cupped hand to my forehead, touch my breast, each shoulder, my heart, and then my lips.

"I rested there a week," I go on. "Your grandmother spread a crazy quilt over me; she called it the quilt of transformation. Your grandmother defended me to my mother. She knew some of the nuns at the convent school at Victoire. She told them that I had miscarried and sent me away to them where she said I'd be safe. You and your father paid dearly for it though."

Annie seems to shift on her pallet. Her voice is small but matter-of-fact: "It was your mother who started the rumours."

"It was all done so secret and hush-like behind curtains and closed doors in the night. None of it tested in the light of day. I've tried to atone."

Annie says nothing. I rush on.

"It divided the town when it happened. There were those who were grateful to your grandmother. But they were no match for religion and by then we had a doctor in town."

"It was your father's baby."

"For a long time, I hated you for knowing. I hated myself." I catch the sobs in my throat.

"I'm sorry." Annie's eyes stare somewhere behind me.

"But you never judged me."

"No." Annie moves her head ever so imperceptibly.

"You were the only one. When you came back to church, at every communion, we would always share a moment, both of us estranged for different reasons. We would look over at each other."

"Yes."

"Your grandmother asked me to name it; to speak to its spirit. She said I should remember it was not to blame. To say good-bye, but I couldn't.

"Your grandmother said the placenta from all the babies was a fertilizer, full of rich vitamins and minerals and that bodies too were rich places. Bones, calcium. That a tree would grow.

"Your grandma had many apple trees, crabapple, many fruit trees, even pear. Her lot, like yours, reached right to the creek bed."

Annie moves. "That and pin cherry and plum. The apple tree is still there."

"She buried the body for me while I watched. Wrapped in a linen cloth, one of her best, she said, from across the sea. We planted a small seedling on the spot, an apple tree. Said it would bear fruit."

Annie looks at me full on. "People would say, a new tree, a new baby. Placentas mostly. A few miscarriages. She was a midwife. But she did what she had to do."

"Some nights I visit in the dark, pay my respects. Pray for its soul."

"Yes, I've felt you there in the night."

"I still have nightmares. 'The Dark Mother,' my own grandmother used to say, 'she who rides the night.' I want to save others from the nightmares. So all these years, Annie, I have prayed to the Holy Mother."

"As have I."

"I have prayed the shame be gone."

"Yes."

"Benedictions and rosaries, I have prayed to make up for my family's sin. I should have named that baby, released its soul."

"You still can. It was your father's shame."

"I know it." I sigh. "Her name is Annie," I say finally.

Daisy reaches over and touches my arm. "Are you all right, Florence?"

That's when I notice there are tears on my cheeks.

ANNIE

Florence looks down, covers her mouth before she makes her confession. That's the only time we've spoken of it.

She has a sign up in her picture window. STOP THE KILLING it says. She's had that sign or some version of it for forty years. She's pro-life. She takes it down every five years or so, cleans it up or replaces it with a new one. She's got a small shrine to Our Lady out front. A fountain and statue, wild rose bushes all around. Sometimes she dresses her in special skirts and veils for feast days. Most people just ignore it. She says she owes her sanity to the Virgin Mary.

"She has forgiven you!" I say as forcefully as I can without rising from the table. My lips don't move but she hears me in her head, as she's heard me through all the washing, through the feel of the water. I can tell from the way her eyes look startled.

That terrible night, we were already in bed; me upstairs, my nana down. This was long after my maman had gone away. On weekends I'd often stay at Nana's and help with whatever was needed. I heard a knock at the back door, propped myself up on one elbow on the bed, parted the curtains and leaned over to look down from my second-storey dormer window to see who was there. I heard my Nana's step on the hall stairs. There was an awful storm out that night, wind and rain, a night the colour of ink, no moon. Still I could hear the choked crying and I could make out a young girl in an old house shift, a blanket over her shoulders, and an over-sized pair of rubber boots. I could hear her sobs and her heaving. I couldn't hear the words, only their timbre, and the slant of her terror in the sharp intake of breath.

When my nana answered, she beckoned the girl inside, took her arm, "Now, that'll be all right."

I had come to the top of the stairs, the girl turned away and hid her face in Nana's shoulder. But I knew her from school, a couple grades ahead of me. She was shaking and there was blood dried on her calves. "Make yourself useful now," Nana had said to me. "We need linens in there. Quick." She pointed to a bedroom off the kitchen we had for the purpose. I brought sheets and blankets and clean towels and started a new fire in the old wood stove. I knew what to do.

When I returned to the kitchen, I found Nana on her knees on top of the counter, rummaging in the back of her Fibber McGee cupboard. She had dug out a quart size canning jar full of dark brown roots, set it on the counter, hoisted herself down onto a chair and opened the lid. Pungent and old, an odour like wet autumn forests wafted across the room. Satisfied, she chose one small root and held it by the tips of her fingers. She placed it on the counter.

"This is dangerous for a woman. Beware how you use it. It speeds labour." She grated a pile just big enough to fill the smallest tea ball.

"Now, go back to bed," she told me, after I had set out the Brown Betty teapot and put the water on to boil.

"And cover your ears. It's a hard thing we have to do tonight. When a girl gets pregnant by one of her blood relations it's a fear-some terrible business, fearsome for the girl, fearsome for the baby.

Some girls cannot bear it. The worst in a family is multiplied —
deformities, defects, and most severe, a deficit of love. The child will
starve from sheer lack of affection. I've seen more than one child
wither that way and die and no one so much as marked its passing."

That's when Nana told me the girl had tried to bring it out with
the sharp end of a coat hanger. That she had hurt herself doing it
and that she may never be able to have babies again. Worst, if she
got an infection, she could die.

"The child has to come out."

I did not sleep the rest of that night.

VERA

It takes us a few minutes to locate the shampoo and when we come
back, we find Florence crying, muttering to herself.

"Take a break," I suggest. But she won't stop washing. "It's my
penance," she says.

"I can't imagine Annie having any scores to settle with you,"
I say.

"The harm wasn't to her," she says. "No, it wasn't to her. It was
the harm I did to myself. Or maybe it was to both of us."

Florence shakes so much that I pour us all a shot of whisky
from the bar and insist she sit down for a minute.

"To Annie, the Water Witcher," I propose.

"Yes," Florence says fiercely, proudly, "to Annie Gallagher, the
best friend I ever had." Florence, Daisy, and I clink our glasses.

But the drink just seems to give Florence verve and she's more
eager than ever to continue. "Let me finish the washing," she insists.
"I have to."

So while Florence washes and Daisy dries, I work over all of
Annie's joints. Flex the wrists, massage the hands to lie flat; the

knees and ankles. Move around the table, massage each arm, and cover it again with the sheet, as if she were alive. We keep unwrapping the body, carefully turning it between us, washing, drying, and massaging it, as if it were a treasure rolled up in a Persian rug we were unfurling.

"She was beautiful wasn't she," says Daisy at last.

"Even at seventy-nine," I agree. "And in such great shape. You'd never know it from all the big clothes she wore," I add.

"I've always loved her white hair," Daisy says.

"The high cheekbones."

"And the skin," Daisy agrees.

"Yup, still smooth, even."

"Why didn't she ever get married?" Daisy looks to Florence.

"Oh!" Florence gives a little hop, like she's been off on a little journey and just come back again.

"Florence?" I ask.

It has been a strange shock, the manner and suddenness of Annie's death.

"I'm sorry," Florence says, smoothing her skirt. It's the kind of big gathered skirt that was popular in the early sixties. The kind my mother used to wear. Still, Florence can't stop. She grabs the bottle of baby shampoo Daisy has put out and starts to work up a lather in her hands. She rubs it into Annie's hair. Between the three of us we manage to rinse Annie's hair and towel it dry. Vera uses the hair blower to finish the job. Annie's hair combs out nicer than when she was living.

"No braids or ribbons," Florence says, when Daisy starts to fix it. "Just comb it and let it hang loose. That's right."

No blush, no eye shadow, no powder, we agree. We file her nails plain, straight across. Buff away all the broken skin on her hands.

I put a thin layer of Vaseline on her lips.

"What's that for?" Daisy wants to know.

"I found it in the cupboard. Keeps them from drying out and puckering."

Florence retrieves the laying out clothes from their shallow box one by one. Together we dress her, turning her, bending her knees to pull on panties, fasten the bra. "The few bras she had," Florence remarks, "did up at the front …"

"That's so sensible," I say.

We slip a sleeve over an arm, button up a red plaid shirt. Daisy and I each take turns holding a leg, while Florence, after careful lifting and turning, slides on a new pair of blue overalls and clips the suspenders on the back, then the front. Blue was Annie's favourite colour. No jewelry, just the ring on her right hand — no one knows from where or why — and a crazy quilt with the tiniest of stitches thrown over the body. And finally, something to cover her face between showings: Florence flourishes a red and white polka dot, OshKosh handkerchief.

"That looks like Annie all right," Daisy pronounces at the end of it.

To keep the forces of decay at bay, Florence puts on the ice machine behind the bar and we collect bucket after bucket of ice cubes and set them out under and around the table at close intervals. Florence switches on the air conditioner — a small unit but it will help — sets the temperature to fifty-five degrees and turns on the fan. That's when she notices the rapping on the back window and gets all nervous again. There's a magpie peeking in.

"Oh, dear," she says. "Annie would want me to see to that."

"What in heaven's name?" Daisy says to me. "What has come over the woman?"

I just shrug.

Five minutes later, when I go to check on her, it sounds like Florence is talking to someone. But it's just a couple of birds on the back deck. She's feeding them.

"I was just telling them that they have to find another restaurant," Florence jokes. But then she makes us close all the drapes before we leave, check all the doors for cracks and find more towels to block leaks of light and air.

All in all, the preparations take about two hours.

Finally, Florence insists that we take the washing water with us.

"It's wash water," Daisy says. "Dirty water. Annie wouldn't want us saving it."

"No, it has to return directly to the earth."

"What?"

"I mean it needs its own special drain, just like the holy water and the consecrated wine at church on Sundays."

"Like Jesus? Well," Daisy says, after she stops the laugh that had begun to rise in her chest, "why don't we take it up to the church then. It's just up the block."

But no, Florence won't hear of the water going near the church, and I give Daisy a warning look.

"It has to be the rose bushes in Annie's own backyard. It has to be those."

"Okay," Daisy and I both say at the same time. Florence has got it in her head and there is no arguing. Daisy, ever the practical one, hauls out a pail from the cleaning closet. "Will this do?"

Florence has to clean it within an inch of its life before we can pour the used water from our basins into it. The three of us make a funny-looking procession with the sun at its highest point overhead, Florence in the lead, Daisy and I taking turns carrying the pail, till we reach the roses, white and pink and yellow, even the odd red, just starting to bud out. Annie's are always earlier than anyone else's. Some say a microclimate, warmer, backing onto the old creek bed, all those old bricks in the soil. The bushes are so tall now, they just about blot out the old brickyard. And I have to admit, they probably need the drink.

ANNIE

Outside the window there are magpies. The three mourners won't notice them right away, but I do. They are missing their peanuts. I strain to hear their family talk. Babies. When the parents are training them, they produce low sounds at the back of their throats "ah eh ah aaaa, ee, ah ee ah ya hmm." And low clicking sounds, like they've lived with the Inuit up on the Arctic circle. They'll make that sound with you too if you feed them.

When they leave the nest, the parents take them on rounds of the town. First the grass. They poke at it unsure of what they're looking for. Hop, hop. Look to their mothers. We all look to our mothers. Then garbage cans and the dump. They learn how to forage in tin and among plastic. How to turn everything over and get the best bits of leftover pizza in the schoolyard or the half-eaten steak out back of the hotel. How to spot a dead ground squirrel on the road. Finally they come to the bird feeders, to sunflower seeds and peanuts, and to us humans.

One pecks at the back window a light rap, a knock. Without turning I know it's Mother Magpie looking in, wanting attention, talking loudly to herself but really she's talking to me the way some people talk while pretending not to. They won't look at you while they are telling you the most intimate details of their lives. Family talk. She is wanting to be fed and I am her nana. I try to greet her. *I can't come right now. I've got company, can't you see?* I do my best to give a little sigh, a shiver. Florence looks up.

I have my tin of peanuts sitting right on the porch by the backdoor, on a weathered, wooden-slat sun chair. Mother Magpie jabbers again, this time louder, swivelling her head with one eye in my direction, fluttering, pausing an instant. She reaches to clean her beak on the windowsill, like a branch, just a small swipe on each side as all birds do just before or after eating, the smallest to the greatest. Her offspring fly up to a nearby limb.

Florence puts down the sponge she was using to wash my body. She goes out the screen door and Mother Magpie flies up and perches on an eave. Florence digs in the tin where the magpie was sitting a moment before. Takes out three peanuts and puts one up on the fence ledge that runs behind the hotel and steps back. Magpie barely hesitates, half hops, half flies, dips her beak, then flies with her prize to the nearest crab apple tree. Barely lands before she starts gabbling again, rolling the peanut over and over in her beak, then her feet, testing it for weight and freshness. Finally bites into it, oohs and aahs softly. Wipes her beak, again, starts to preen her feathers. Florence steps back slowly, leaves another handful on the top of the nearest post. The birds swoop down in turns, carrying more peanuts off, one at a time, to eat and to hide.

The sun is a fiery orange out the back, the thunderclouds all but gone. I watch from my new perch, which is everywhere now, eyes in the back of my head. In a minute the magpie leaves, on to its other rounds, the schoolyard, the main hardtop highway just the other side of town. Florence comes inside, picks up her sponge and squeezes the water out again, gently. She looks at me carefully, her head at an angle, but I don't meet her gaze.

I don't remember the day my mother left. All I remember is that she was like a ghost at the window staring out hour after hour, in a white night dress to the knee, her black hair tangled, long past her waist. Her face dark. Her eyes a deep brown the opposite of mine and my father's, our eyes blue and our hair yellow. She was ravishing. My maman was French. My father's parents, Cornish Irish. That is when we still had the brickworks. Nana Gallagher had to come to cook for us at night. She tried herbs on my maman, healing teas. Maman kept saying she herself had made a mistake. She took her tea dutifully and shook her head and kept repeating, "I am mistaken. Taken by mystery, I am." The tea helped her sleep for a time.

There were only two small windows in our little house. Maman paced from one to the other, singing to herself and watching. She would tell me she was waiting for a special visitor. A neighbour would rap on the front door but she wouldn't move. Not this one, *ma petite*, she told me. The priest would stop by and she would turn her head away from his knocking. Nor this one, she said, and she would put fingers to my lips until the knocking ceased.

And then she was gone. When they were in their cups, the old people used to say to my father that she'd fallen in love with the leader of a brass band and escaped to the west coast.

I was there when she first opened the door to him. A Lebanese pedlar who played the accordian and made the rounds of the towns with his cloth, his thread, and his spices, his visions of the Old World. My father was at the brickworks stoking the fires, as he often was, days and nights at a time. The music worked a spell on her; she became possessed by the dark-haired man. From then on, she told me to watch for him; him and only him we allowed to enter.

I grew to love those visits and that man for how happy he made her, how much light she carried in her body when she was around him. And I grew to hate him when she was gone, for the opposite reason, the darkness that fell around us, my father, my nana, and me.

I took that nightshirt everywhere after she left, bundled up like a doll or a teddy bear, wore it to bed with me, would not let it be laundered.

For a few years, she sent money. Envelopes postmarked from all over the world. Wrapped in blank letter paper with three words roughly marked: *pour ma fille,* for my daughter. Currency with exotic colours and faces from far off lands, that no banks in Majestic or Victoire could cash.

5

FATHER PAT

Florence phoned me at the rectory this morning just after break-fast. Then Daisy, then Vera. The three furies. Like they planned it. Wanting me to meet them at the hotel after lunch, to book a Christian burial for the body of Annie Gallagher. In the seminary they said on my final field evaluation, *Tends to passivity. Needs to work on self-confidence.* I am not passive when it comes to leader-ship. I'm not afraid to speak up. I can say no.

No, no, no, I said three times.

"She never took communion and she never came for confession. She set herself apart. How can I bury her?"

"Yes, she was there. She rose and she sat and she kneeled at the appointed times. But her mouth never moved, nor her feet."

One time I asked her why she didn't partake with the rest of us; she gave me a cryptic answer. "My hands won't let me."

"She was in church every Sunday. She was *a member* of this Christian community. I don't know about *a leader*," I said.

"No," I repeated. "No. I'm sorry for your loss."

But I couldn't say No to the meeting. Now it is past lunch and we are standing in the lobby at the hotel.

"The new rubric is—"

"I know the new rubric, Father," Vera interrupts. I ignore her.

"That we don't eulogize the person as much as their Christian life and celebrate our belief in the resurrection of Jesus Christ. I'm reluctant to give someone a full church burial whose communion status is irregular."

"That's just it, Father. She lived it." Vera folds her arms and digs in her heels. "She didn't just show up on Sundays."

"She had a drinking problem, I've heard. Among other things."

"Oh, Father, that was almost thirty years ago, now, according to the oldtimers. Besides, we all have our pasts." Daisy fixes me with a big smile. I can instantly feel my cheeks flush. Of course. Everyone knows. They all live in each other's back pockets out here. But I won't be intimidated from my duty.

"Don't you see? She chose to excommunicate herself! She didn't trust anyone with her reasons. She didn't seek forgiveness."

"She didn't have the benefit of a deathbed confession, Father." Florence straightens up.

"I would be going against her will."

"But who knows the heart, Father?" Daisy Goodchild, smile gone, all innocence.

"She wouldn't meet my eyes. She never stopped to visit."

"Well, I don't know, Father, she met everyone else's eyes." Florence gives me the once over. "Maybe she was trying to show respect? You know in the old days how women were taught not to meet the gaze of a priest...."

All I know of Annie is what I've witnessed. Her striding between the hotel and the church every Sunday. And all those cats she kept out back of her house, on the roof, around the yard, on the picnic table out front as well as that family of magpies. Someone else seems to be feeding them now. If it's true about the drinking, I don't know how she kept the hotel all those years without relapsing.

"She had cats," I say out loud.

"What's wrong with cats, Father?" Daisy narrows her eyes as she says it.

"Dozens of them." I can't help myself. No one believes in witches anymore, least of all me, still I can't help myself. I realize I was a little afraid of her.

"What is wrong with you, Father?" Florence Enders is staring at me, her hands firmly planted on her hips.

"Well, she was out witching or whatever you call it. Doesn't sound particularly Christian!"

"She did all kinds of good for this community, Father." Daisy juts out her chin and waves her arms in the air. "Wells for twenty miles around. And that young girl. She took in that young girl, Father, in her time of need. Your altar girl."

"Not for long."

"What do you mean 'not for long?'" Florence elbows her way into the fray again.

"I mean it's not appropriate for this young girl to be on the altar in her — condition."

"She's baptized and had her first communion in this very church."

"Years ago, I understand."

"She's enrolled in confirmation class for fall already."

"There are a number of irregularities in this parish which I've overlooked under the circumstances. The girl altar servers, the excess of lay preaching and presiding. I have to draw the line on this."

"But Father, the Vatican approved girls for altar service almost ten years ago!"

"Approved but never mandated; the local pastor, as presider at the liturgy, has the final decision."

"Annie had every intention of helping Kelsey get a start with her baby. Now it's up to those of us who remain. You included. Are you a pro-lifer, Father, or are you not?"

"Of course, but this is not a matter of pro-life or not pro-life, Florence. I've been tolerating the situation on the altar till the church closes. But with the bishop coming out ... and now this death...."

"We have no boys who want to serve on the altar, Father," Vera says quietly.

"And it's no wonder! They see a girl up there.... Boys at that age.... It's completely irregular!"

Florence takes a step forward and looks me right in the eye: "You're what's irregular here."

"Oh, all right! I'll give Annie a church funeral if you agree to have the wake at the church as well."

For a moment, Florence hesitates, frowns. "Father, if it were me, I'd agree with you, but this hotel is Annie's second home. People knew her here. They came and took their coffee here and picked up their mail. They got the news. That is the nature of a public house. It's not just a drinking establishment."

"It's — it's so undignified! A wake at a bar. And for some, just an excuse for excess."

"Her body is in the next room, Father. Can you stand beside it and say that?"

"Fine. I'll do the wake if you promise not to serve any alcohol."

"Not till the end of the evening and then only in moderation."

I can't help but sigh. "Meanwhile, you should be praying for her soul. And there'll be no Eucharist since she didn't avail herself of communion when she was alive." I turn towards the bar, meaning to go visit the deceased.

"Oh, but there will be prayers, Father…. The glorious, the sorrowful and the joyful mysteries. One of each in the morning, afternoon and evening tomorrow. The Catholic Women's League has it all organized. A wake, Friday night, and a Liturgy of the Word, as you say, for the funeral which you or the bishop will celebrate on Saturday."

Perhaps my face betrays my disbelief. Annie a devotee of Mary?

"Oh, Annie was a great devotee of Our Lady. She often said she owed her recovery from the drink to her. Had shrines set up inside the house and around the garden."

But that wasn't the end of it. Another half hour of haggling before they finally let me perform my priestly office and bless the body.

DAISY

We decide the three of us to go back to the hotel after lunch and meet the priest together to haggle about the wake.

"Several of the parishioners want to say a few words, Father," I start, giving him my best smile.

"Well," he says, "they'll have to wait till I'm done the service."

"Nonsense, Father," says Florence. "The vigil is the place for stories about the deceased."

Vera is more diplomatic. "According to the rubric, Father, the vigil is the place for the bereaved to express their grief."

The man looks like a strange bird floating around in those heavy black robes summer and winter. I can't help but think he could use some style coaching. This is Majestic, after all, the middle of oil Alberta not Europe in the Middle Ages! Trousers have been in style for four hundred years.

Oh, word gets around. There's more going on in that heart under those cassocks than he lets on. There isn't much you can keep to yourself in a place like this. There's always some story with the priests they send us. Majestic is a backwater. Nobody chooses us.

Florence dares him to go in and say his intentions in front of the body. He struts and he preens and straightens his clerical collar before marching us in like a small parade to the Table of Truth. Father Pat sniffs when he sees the rose Vera found on Annie's person, sitting in a small bowl of water beside her head. Then he spots the suspenders above the top of the quilt (the crazy quilt we found on her bed), spots the farmer's shirt and wonders at the choice of resting clothes we have given her.

"Are those hers?"

"Yes, the very same," Florence tells him.

"What about dressing her—" He hesitates, but we all know what is coming, "prop—" He catches himself. "In a more appropriate manner."

"Do you mean like a lady?" I say loudly, drawing out the last word. I think about suggesting he donate something from his wardrobe. Size him up. Nope. Too skinny in the hips.

"She didn't own a skirt, Father," Vera says evenly.

"Surely one of you must have something to donate to the cause."

The three of us look at each other. For heaven's sakes! What a maddening man.

"It didn't seem right to put her in a dress," Vera says with just the right amount of deference.

"She worked all her life, more a man's work than a woman's," I snort.

"Bad luck to dress a dead person in someone else's clothes," Florence agrees.

"We did find a rosary in her things and put that in her hands," I offer with as much innocence as I can muster.

But that only makes Father Pat's face darken and twist. You can see that he wants to say something, but he gains control of himself, as if he's reminding himself that the church is closing, after all, and this is one last cross to bear.

FLORENCE

Daisy and two others from the local Catholic Women's League toil the rest of the day to get the hotel in shape. They work with shirt sleeves rolled up in the cool air, careful not to disturb the body and to keep the doors and windows closed. They wash the floors and all the curtains. Change the buckets of ice around the table. Give everything a good once over.

I'd forgotten the place is all pine inside. The floor, one of those properly sprung for dancing, when they still had bands and dances at the hotel, and it was the thing to do on a Saturday night. Everyone used to bring their children, lay them under a bench with a blanket, let them fall asleep to big band swing and old time music, dance till four in the morning and not feel tired. We used to have a twelve-piece brass band in these parts, amateur theatre every winter. That's something else we've lost. The bounce in our step, the heel and toe of pure celebration. People coming together around seasons: summer weddings, harvest balls, New Year's Eve dances, spring teas. Time was a going concern.

ANNIE

My father's job in the Great War was to guide the packhorses to the front lines. The ones carrying ammunition, guns. Almost all of the horses met their deaths eventually. He said their chances of survival were worse than the common foot soldier. He went to sleep and woke to the sounds of their dying in his head. No amount of coaxing could fool them. They all followed his voice, worked for him out of raw sacrifice, the knowledge of friends facing death together. There was no other explanation for it.

My maman told me the *Canadiens* were shier on the front, more polite than the Americans, not so forward as the British. She told me how my father put her finger on a big empty map of North America and guided her hand. *"Ici,"* he said, "up in the northwest corner." How it was hundreds of miles from any city markers, a long flat plain. "This," he said, "this is my land. It's got good clay, the best for bricks. Just on the edge of town."

Where she was from the hills were made of clay too, but they grew wheat, oats, and orchards. Or did once.

"What grows?" she pressed him.

"Barley," he said, "and cattle. Potatoes, carrots, and beets."

"But so far from any water, so far north?"

"Oh, there's water. Plenty of it. We'll live right up against a brook and there are wells everywhere."

"Are there any vineyards?" she asked him.

He laughed. "No, none of that."

"Or almonds?"

"Maybe at Christmas."

Almond trees, she meant, she told me. The fragrance of their white buds in spring. The hills filled with yellow-skinned plums, pears, and apple orchards, beech, boxwood, and wild geranium. Fields of tomato, wheat.

He told her they could have an apple tree if she wanted it. A pear might survive if they were careful.

What kind of place had she agreed to come where fruit might not grow?

When they arrived that first August, there was an apple tree already growing in the yard that gave a small, hard, stinging fruit. All seed, hardly a mouthful, that made you grimace with the tartness. "Crab apple," my father told her. "Not fit for eating." Yet this is what they used to make their jelly and cider.

6

KRISTIAN

I come back to town on foot and hang around all day Thursday, giving the hotel a wide pass. I see an ambulance deliver the body through the front door and some women coming in and out.

A scruffy magpie hops from tree to tree while I walk the block from the church to the hotel and the schoolyard and back again. He's probably a baby — doesn't even have all his head feathers yet. And then it comes to me. The nosy magpie at the meth shack. You don't happen to have any relatives east of town? He gives a low whirring sound almost like the purr of a cat and the colour of sadness, a dull brown. I try to shake him then and start in the direction of the old brickyard.

I don't feel like eating, just thirsty, but I refuse to drink. Maybe I'll die too, I think and that would be all right, because I've really screwed up this time, haven't I?

Andy is long gone, said he was done with the drug running business, said he was disappearing for a few weeks, maybe Vancouver, maybe Highway 101 all the way down to San Diego, as far as he could go till this whole thing blows over. This situation just weirded him out. There was no trace of her under the wheels when we checked later, but we saw her and she was dead.

I see things different than most. I see colours around people. I see colours when I hear music. Even words, names or numbers, when I see them or hear them, have colours. The number five is the colour of mustard. The letter A is dark red. Though mostly I try to turn off that part of my brain and pretend I see and hear like everyone else.

That's why I like meth. Not the way it affects other people. All the altered perceptions, the distorted shapes and sounds, the vivid colours. With me it's the opposite. Weird but not weird, if you know what I mean. Everything toned down. I still see colours but so does everyone else. I feel normal. Calm. That's what's got me into this trouble.

On the road she was swathed in white light. It was swirling around her. I've never seen white light around anything before and it scares me. I don't know what it means. I don't know how I'm going to tell Kelsey about any of this.

I met Kelsey Sands at a party. She has a good light about her too, a kind of purplish red, like the fuchsia my mom used to grow on the front porch when she was alive, only stronger. Kelsey's into all these causes: environmentalism, clean up the Tar Sands, clean up the air, the rivers. She's smart, eh, and artistic. Says she wants to be a fashion designer once she gets her high school.

That first night I tell her all kinds of jokes to keep her laughing. Hey, my mind goes a hundred miles a minute, sometimes I talk my face off, but if I'm amped, I can really be funny. All the connections slow down.

She's doing ecstasy. You should try meth, I tell her. More intense, more focused.

The second time we go out, I bring her some crank and we make out. She really likes it. And then she gets pregnant and she won't touch the stuff anymore or me either. I am such a loser.

On my last round of the town, the curtains on the hotel are shut, and there is a lettered sign on the door: CLOSED UNTIL FURTHER NOTICE, and below that a printed message that says "Annie Gallagher has passed away and the wake will be Friday, viewing during the day and service at seven at night. Funeral rites on Saturday at two o'clock. Residents should note that this may be the last funeral held in St. Joseph's Catholic Church in Majestic as the church is closing. Everyone is welcome."

KELSEY

When I see Miss Florence waiting at the school bus stop in Majestic, the baby gives a little kick inside and I know. "What's wrong? Where's Annie?" I ask coming down the last step, holding my stomach with one hand and the railing with the other.

"There's been an accident," Miss Florence says. But even then I know that there's more to it.

"Where are we going?" I ask.

"You're staying with me for now," Florence murmurs.

"But why?"

"We can go to Annie's later and get a few things if you like. First, let me take you back to my kitchen and fix you a cup of tea," she finishes cryptic-like.

She keeps me talking by asking about school and teachers, teasing me about when I was in grade one, how I'd learned to read right away, how I loved my books. She was my teacher.

The trees seem to reach out while we talk, the new leaves, so green, play with the light in the breeze. I am careful to walk over and around the cracks in the crumbling sidewalk that runs through the centre of Majestic and all around the grade school, all the way to Florence's house. I resist the urge to circle the horse chestnut tree that guards Miss Florence's gate with its yellow-winged seed pods, the only tree of its kind in town. I mark how the orange tiger lilies are blooming around Our Lady at the corner shrine. I walk up Miss Florence's front path, past the statue of Mary and notice all the garden gnomes in her yard, the birdbath, the old two-seater swing, like my mom's, only with mom's the paint is chipped and faded. I see that one of the lilac bushes in her yard is in bloom. I mark these small details all down in my head not knowing why but knowing from the way Miss Florence avoids a direct gaze, the way she diverts my questions and a certain sadness to her voice, a faraway look, that something bad has happened.

Miss Florence's kitchen is done in cornflower blue, bordered in striped yellow wallpaper that is fading in places, an apple tree looking in through the back window, blossoming white. All I can think is that for such a plain person, Miss Florence has the prettiest kitchen.

The water is on and in no time boiled, the tea steeping. She starts by saying that she has to remind me that no matter her news, I have to think of the child first. That is the way it is with mothers. She pours the tea and waits till I've had a sip, before she tells me about Annie.

ANNIE

Yes, I have scars. The second year I was at the institution, they pulled me out of the kitchen where I was scrubbing vegetables and ushered me into a room. Three people sat at the front behind a table. There was a chair facing them, set several feet back. The ward lady pointed. "Go, sit."

I looked at her. "Who are—?" but with a jerk of the arm she stopped me mid-sentence. I was always asking questions and always in trouble for it. She steered me to the chair and set me down. She left and I faced the panel alone. One was a lady with a fur-trimmed hat that nearly danced above her dull brown suit. I knew it for a red fox fur of the kind that the boys used to trap at home. Another was a man in a green tweed suit. The other, in a white coat, was the institution's physician. I smiled when I saw him in the room. He did our annual check-ups and was often in and out to check on sick residents. He was a gentle man.

I started towards him. "I'm all right, Doctor Williams, aren't I?"

"Just take a seat, Annie," he said. "All in good time."

And I sat back down, tried to smooth the corners of my apron, the hem of my skirt.

"That a girl. These two people have a few questions for you."

The lady said Good morning to me.

"Good morning, Ma'am."

They had a file folder in front of them. They were passing it back and forth, reading it out loud.

"Found sleeping in the beds of other inmates."

"Male or female?"

"Both it would appear. She doesn't discriminate."

"So far nothing untoward reported. Just sleeping, surely seeking comfort, the warmth of a human body," the man in the tweed suit was saying.

"The Superintendent feels it's only a matter of time," said the lady with the hat.

I liked her hat. It reminded me of my mother's best hat. Like throwing cares to the wind that hat, so puffed up, such flair. I had never met the Superintendent. He travelled around the school with a couple of orderlies in tow.

"Natural urges," agreed the doctor. "A common by-product of institutional life."

"Have you ever been promiscuous?" asked the lady with the hat, looking at me directly this time.

"I don't know," I said. I didn't know what the word meant.

"'Below average intelligence' too it says here."

"Trouble in school."

"Teacher says she never learned how to read."

"Yes."

"The first stumbling block on the path to moral decay, gentlemen."

The tweed man cleared his throat. "She is very attractive, almost in a primitive way," the man said as if he were trying out a new theory. He pronounced "primitive" as if it were a code for something.

"Well," the doctor looked me up and down, finding me not a child anymore, and I found myself crossing my arms over my breasts. "Perhaps, but surely...."

The lady caught him blushing. "She is very desirable, isn't she, Doctor?" The doctor kept staring straight ahead, red-faced.

"Thank you," he said. "That will be all, Annie."

He pressed a button and the attendant came to fetch me.

Months later they sent me to Ponoka and said I had to get my appendix out.

But I knew it wasn't my appendix.

One of our neighbours, old Mrs. Granger had died of appendicitis before the doctor could get to her. She came to my grandma to get help for the pain. She was screaming, worse than a woman in labour — there was no ebb or flow, no stopping it. Nana took a willow switch and shaved off bits of bark and made a tea for her.

"There must be a mistake," I told the nurse in the ambulance. "I'm not sick."

"No, Dr. Williams is confident of it." But she bit her lip when she said it and looked away. And when they put the restraints on me going into the operating room, just like they did every night at the training school, and the nurses held me down tighter than need be and they put the mask of ether to my face, I knew something was not right.

7

KRISTIAN

When I finally get home the Old Man says to me, "Where have you been all day?"

"None of your business," I say.

"As long as you live in this house, you are my business! Where were you this morning."

"Huff and puff and blow your house down!" I tell him. Old-red-in-the-face.

"What you running around in the dark for, Son? I see trouble in your eyes."

"Leave me alone," I say to him and make a beeline for my room.

"The people in town talk. Don't think I don't know what they say. And that girl. Do you have anything to do with that girl, the one that's pregnant?"

"Screw off!" I slam the door in his face and lock it. Just then my phone rings. It's been ringing all day. The Man in Black. Probably wants to know where the product is. In a ditch off the side of a highway? Dumped in an ocean? I don't know! I keep looking at the phone and then putting it back in my pocket again. The third time I cut the ring short, turn it off, and throw it across the room.

The old man shouts again, "And where did you get that phone? Tell me the truth!"

"Annie Gallagher is dead," I shout back. "Annie Gallagher is dead!" I hear a pause and then a shuffling of feet on the other side of the door, and then, nothing.

I try to sleep but I keep dreaming of the crash on the road, the witch's last words and my mom's face before she died, how she was always smiling.

By the time I surface out of my hideyhole the next morning, the sun is high in the sky and the Old Man's truck is gone to feed the cattle. I don't stop for anything: toilet, breakfast, or shower. I walk into town.

At Main I see the street lined with half-ton trucks and cars of all descriptions. Like it was for Mom's funeral. I catch a cry in my throat. Everyone said how young she was. So many hands touching me all at once, pumping my arm, punching my shoulder, ruffling my hair. Lips saying "Sorry, sorry, sorry," over and over again, "you poor kid," and then nothing. The long silence. Like the day was swallowed up in itself and nobody could talk about it anymore.

I see the women walking in loose, chattering groups up the street with plates of food in their hands, and it dawns on me how hungry I am and how much I'm shaking. My body hurts in every spot. I duck into an alley, take a quick piss, search for a quiet backyard and a coiled up garden hose. I turn on the tap and try to wash my hands and face. Slap my hair into place and think about how I might slip into the hotel, how even a cup of coffee might steady me.

Every year my maman would mark the *Fête des Rois* with us, Epiphany, the Feast of the Three Kings. She fashioned me a gold crown from the foil of an old chocolate box. Set it on my head and I was queen for the day. She baked a cake for me, a strange pastry really, that called for *frangipane:* almond paste layered between the pastry with a dry bean hidden in it. She used marzipan because it was all she could get from the local German shopkeeper and mixed it with butter and eggs to make a cream.

"Chew carefully, *ma petite,*" she would say. *"Regarde le fève."* Watch for the bean.

I was always queen those first years before maman went away. Before she turned sad. Before her gardens died. Only the bean survived, whose seed she had mail-ordered all the way from Toronto, whose vines she had laboured over. Even the nuns at Victoire couldn't master the *fève.*

Nana said Maman had small orange and lemon trees growing in the windows, seeds she first husbanded from gifts, but the winter dark killed them all eventually. They miss *le soleil* she would say to me. They miss their *maman soleil.* Her seventh winter of seed ordering, she left. I was only five.

So when the oranges came that first Christmas without her, I knew who they were from, we all knew, though we pretended not to. I tore into the box, gorged myself, ate six in an hour before Nana found me in the potato bin in the basement. The perfume of citrus on my hands, filling the air. I pushed the box towards Nana, wiped my mouth with the back of my hand, wiped my hands on my dress. The juice so sweet. I would not change that dress for days. The smell of my maman.

They begin arriving at the hotel Friday about ten o'clock – the usual time they arrive for the mail. The bell on the door rings when it opens. The men wipe their boots at the threshold, crowd in, take off their ball caps, their Stetsons. All the grain companies of the world are represented in those hats: United Grain Growers, Wheat Pool, Monsanto, Cargill, Agrium. The women follow cautiously, bearing sweets and sandwiches, straining to see into the next room. Some of them have never been beyond the mail wicket, the coffee shop and into the bar. Even the men hesitate to cross the boundary between vestibule and beer parlour today, till Jack sits himself down by Annie's head, hat on his knee, hands crossed on the head of his cane.

A hush falls around the body as the first mourners gather. A hush and a hallow. At first, some are startled by her open eyes but then their eyes rest on the flowers. The roses from her garden bunched up in vases all around the room show lovely against the white linens of the bier. We cut as many as we could find. The air is heady with their fragrance. Mike pulls out his video camera, shoots close-ups of the flowers and the bier. The men said they wanted to record this for posterity.

The mourners dip their heads to Annie, to me, to each other, "Sorry for your loss," they say. I nod and take their coats. "Coffee's on in the bar today," I tell the men and motion for them to help themselves. I tell the ladies they're needed in the kitchen, and they seem to understand. Suddenly no more fuss and nonsense, they are there to serve lunch.

"A perfectly fine day for seeding," cracks Buster. The other guests laugh nervously. People are late this year, waiting for moisture.

"Good luck to plant on the day of a burial. Good crops," someone else says. And that's how the men come to gather in one corner of the pub, around Jack, just south of Annie's feet.

ALEX

I spend my time attending — auctions, funerals, news on the radio, weather reports. I attend orientations on new agricultural regulations, stock breeder certifications, municipal planning. It's all the same. Sometimes eleven at night or one in the morning, I pull in to home. Doesn't matter. They're what keep me going. Other farmers, the only people who understand why I stay on the land.

What's at stake? Waking up every morning to wind, birdsong, sunrise. Neighbours, family, roots. My grandparents' homestead. All the oceans they crossed, the labours, the droughts, hoppers, hailstorms, the failed crops. They left everyone and everything to come out here alone, for a life of hope, a real home. I'd be no better off than those poor buggers that drift from bed to bed in the city at night, from heating grate to shelter, from cardboard to shopping cart. Majestic and these farmers are the only family I have.

Bob's a study in the future: city slicker turned gentleman farmer. After his wife died he turned right strange. Sold his business. Built a bigger greenhouse, the old one small and makeshift, just some recycled windows jigsawed together. This new one is state of the art, engineered with special plastic and fans for ventilation. The size of a large machine shed.

He tells me he and Virginia used to watch for roses on trips. If she saw something, they'd stop and take cuttings. Might have been in the middle of southern Ontario or the coast of California. He would tease her, "Are you sure these are going to grow in northern Alberta?" She'd laugh. She kept the clippings alive in disposable coffee cups refilled with fresh water every morning. That was how she grew the roots. He got so he started to pick them up on his home reno jobs too, anything exotic. She'd grow it inside the first year or two, wait till it rooted, bloomed, decide if she wanted to keep it or not.

He's tried to keep everything the way it was. The house. The yard. Even the fence: the weathered posts and barbed wire rusted, but patched with new in places. He waters and fertilizes like she would have, took up where she left off. He sent to Manitoba for Morden hardies, to Ontario for some breed they call the Explorers. Mail ordered to Britain and China, tea roses by the bucket full. All roses. Darned if I know one from the other, but he knows all their names. Genus, species, Latin this and Latin that. Special permits and passes and customs arrangements. Took delivery of the roots via Canada Post in February, nursed them along inside his green-house. This spring he's been spending all his free time in the garden, hoeing and weeding and transplanting. Wants to turn the whole yard into one giant rose garden. It's why Annie ended up there. All he needed, he said, was one more good well. Puts bird feeders out everywhere on his property, summer and winter; peanuts for the bigger birds. Bet he's never seen a magpie peck out the eyes of a newborn calf. "Waste of good soil," I said to Annie at the post office last week, "this love affair he's got with the roses and the birds."

"Oh, but what a beautiful affair, Alex, don't you think?"

MIKE

I pan the room as people arrive, one by one, zoom in as they come near the body, leave flowers, cards. Some cry, some remain stoic. If you lean close, you will catch a few words of the women in the kitchen. The talk is all about Annie, something she'd said to them, some way she had helped them. "What was that story about her early life? Where was she sent off to?" one of them asks. Just then, one of the guys yells at me from the other side of the room, teasing-like but serious too, "Are you getting 'er all down?" and a sign that they want to be recorded too. I move over to their corner, train the camera on Bob, who's so upset he doesn't even notice at first.

"I feel sick," he's saying to them. "I know Annie's death is my fault." He stabs his thigh over and over again as he's saying it. "It was fork lightning, miles away at first, but she was determined to finish the job. And then it came on all of a sudden. I should have insisted!"

"She was as deaf as a post," Alex interjects.

"As blind as an earwig," says Buster.

"As stubborn—" Jack gives a sharp intake of breath, "as an ox," he finishes, eyes cast down.

Bob demonstrates now how he waved his arms, jumped up and down, the lightning crackling all around like a battlefield show. The birds still hawking bugs. The air not moving. "She didn't see it coming."

"Terrible bad luck," Buster chews on his cold pipe.

"The more the gift, the more the loss," says Alex.

"The more the love, the more the loss, you mean," says Jack in a long drawn out hollow voice, barely audible, as if echoing over a distance.

We all let our glances fall on him, wondering about the catch in his voice, everyone except Bob, who needs to keep talking.

"I called the ambulance right away. Gave her mouth to mouth. Couldn't think of what else to do."

"A strong well she found you," Alex says. "Flags still standing where the lightning struck. Thick, lots of doubles."

"She fell forward, but crouching." Bob demonstrates from his chair. "Nothing broken." He goes on to explain how if she'd been holding herself straight, chances were the lightning would have entered through her head. As it is the lightning went direct to the heart, right through the artery. Quicker that way, according to the doctor. "She died instantaneously." Bob bites his lip, grimaces, the way men are bound to do when they are pained to the point of tears but don't want to cry.

"At least she didn't suffer," Alex says.

Everyone nods.

"She was getting up there," offers Buster. "'Spect I'll be joining her one of these days," and he raps his knuckles three times on the corner of Annie's table.

"Those kids were out on the road again," Alex says, "right where it happened. As soon as the lightning started to hit, they skedaddled."

"Usually Daisy spies the SUV when it passes through," says Buster. "But no sign of it yesterday."

"I've seen them do the drops early, once a week, every week," Alex continues. "Parked and waiting on the road out front. Could set my watch by it."

"Bea, at the gas station tells Daisy they stop on occasion. Always pay in cash, big bills. None of it counterfeit yet, but she feels better when she's seen the back of them."

Alex leans forward now and lowers his voice. "I'm feeding the animals or working in the fields. Sometimes they sit there for hours till finally an SUV steals up the road. Two guys get out, one opens the hatch, the other guy shoves a package in the back. Sometimes they exchange a parcel for a cardboard box. Sometimes I just see a box in the ditch. No one has to tell me, 'Don't touch.'"

"Right out on my quarter mile?" Bob grips both his knees.

"That's one of them," Alex jerks his head back, and the group all turns to look at the young kid sitting by himself in the opposite corner, folding his baseball cap as if he were trying to make a paper airplane out of it. "Kristian. Hans Mueller's son."

"No use calling the RCMP."

None of them take their eyes off him.

I point the camera in that direction, zoom in. Kristian looks away quickly, looks down. I zoom back to the Table of Truth, Alex, Buster, and Jack in the lens.

"Ever since the Mrs. died," Alex is saying, "the old man's never been right in the head. Like he lost his reason for living. The boy's just left to roam the farm, the roads. He goes to class when he feels like it. 'Why isn't he in school?' I ask his old man one day when I'm over and I see Kristian walking around the yard with music plugged into his ears. 'Kristian doesn't need school. He's got the farm,' he says to me. Between us and the pillar there, he's no farm boy."

"No indeedy." Buster laughs and slaps his knee. "Doesn't know the top of a pail from its bottom and that's no word of a lie."

"Well, he's smart enough. Built himself a little shack in the barnyard. Insulated, wired, even hooked up to the well." Alex goes on. "I don't know what he's got cooking up over there, but it sure stinks."

Bob has started to sweat. "A little shack? What do you mean?"

"Keeps pretty strange company for a country boy," Buster says, untangling his tooled leather boots from each other, leaning forward and grinding his right toe into the hardwood floor for punctuation. "Those devil-fingered friends of his like their little black fast cars. Ride awfully delicate on our gravel."

"Yeah, that and their white-walled SUVs." You can tell Alex is wanting to spit as he says it.

"The ones that pass through town are rough-looking customers all right, tattoos up and down their arms. Devil skulls on their fists, knuckle breakers."

By the time I pan the room again, the kid has abandoned the paper airplanes. Now he's wringing his cap with his hands, over and over again, holding it up as he twists it, as if he's studying it for something. I remember now when the Mueller family used to attend Church, before the mother died, how Kristian could never sit still.

"Yeah, I was over to the Mueller farm last week," Buster says, lowering his voice, "talking to the old man about borrowing his bull.

"'What do you feed your wildlife?' I asked him. 'Quite the odour.' He ignored me, kept squinting into the sun. The guy can hardly stand straight anymore. He uses a walking stick; one of his legs is buggered. Says his ticker's offbeat. Wouldn't be surprised if one of these days it's his funeral we're attending."

"I've asked him about the smoke coming out of the pumphouse." It was Alex's turn again. "That's what he calls the shack. Struck me as right strange. 'What are you curing in there?'

"He said he didn't know. It was some experiment Kristian had to do for the school."

"Yeah, the land is full of experiments these days." Buster presses the crease on the top of his Stetson with one hand.

Alex leans forward again. "I tell you, I've never felt this way before, but I feel fear living here now."

Bob moves to the edge of his chair. "What do you mean?"

"Someone's been dipping into my fertilizer tank. Leaves the cap off sometimes. The dog stays under the porch, doesn't even bark. I'm not sure what they do to get past her. Lucky the wind's been from the right direction."

"Who would be crazy enough to do that?"

"Must be someone you know to get by the dog."

"And I know a lot. Probably every kid ten miles in four directions has been my summer help at one time or another. None of them stayed long. Too much work, not enough money."

"It's getting so you can't leave anything unlocked anymore." Buster shakes his head. "Can't trust your neighbour. If they can move it and it don't talk, it's fair game."

Alex keeps his eyes on the kid. "There were foot tracks by the tank," Alex continues. "Fingerprints where the hose had gone in. Certain tire treads. I have my suspicions."

"Hans Mueller's probably the most afraid of us all," Jack says suddenly as the old man comes through the door.

"Still," Bob manages finally to get a word in edgewise, "Kristian's got every right to pay his respects. If he was out there yesterday morning like you said, he'd have seen the whole show, and I bet it would have shook him up." He grimaces hard as he says it, and you know he's talking about himself as much as anyone.

Jack says nothing. Shifts his posture from time to time but mostly keeps an eye on Annie.

ANNIE

I was walking Bob Taylor's front garden, near the road, zigzagging, making my rounds. I had told him to go to the back garden and stay there. He's always got so many questions. I need all my powers of concentration for this, I told him.

I was listening for the rush of the water beneath me, the roaring of oceans in my ears. I was attentive to the stirring of the waters inside me like I always am when I'm witching, following the streams like I am wont to do, leaning into the earth, maybe more so because of these trying days, compensating for the distraction of the bishop's coming. I didn't notice the charged air rising. Only that my bones were aching — a sign that rain was close. I could smell it, but it was nothing that would hurt the witching. So I widened my radius, followed a path like a spiral, looking for the centre at the edges, looking for the source.

I had said to Bob when we arranged this, "The full moon is not for another two weeks," the days either side of it, the best time for planting and for finding water — that's when the waters are highest, like the tide. The force field, strongest.

But Bob didn't want to wait. "Now's the time to be putting in the roses, to establish their roots," he said. They need a long season the first year and for that he needed water.

"You're going to have to get electric fences," I said, when I got there, "to keep out the deer and the hares."

"That and more," he'd agreed.

Then he saw the thunderheads and he got worried.

"No matter," I told him. "It's a long ways off. Can't but help the wand, give it a little extra tug." Still, a freak of nature so early in the morning. One that I marked as a portent of the times we're living in, when the weathers are all mixed up, the air currents confused between times of year and times of day.

He offered me shelter, nervous suddenly, a cup of coffee, and a later start.

"Water is witched best at the break of day," I reminded him, "and anyways, that storm is still a distance." That's when I sent him behind the house.

The moment the bolt hit, I had a vision of the world laid new on the land, the fields flooded as far as the eye could see. A vision that I've only had a couple of times in the flesh, when by a peculiar trick of the season, the ground stayed frozen through a cool spring, heavy winter snows lay thawing, pooling slowly on the surface, water on the prairie as wide as an ocean. People might have believed they were saved, that a miracle covered everything, that the drought had been reversed by God, global warming trumped. But the older ones knew the trick. A northern mirage. Everything makes its way into the ground eventually.

That morning, in the middle of an early day thunderstorm, I knew it was a vision of the end.

Did it hurt? Just a prick of the skin, a split second and then I was flying.

BUSTER GOODCHILD

I've been keeping an eye on the young fellow off in the corner by himself, the one who looks like he hasn't slept in days. I've heard enough of Daisy's side of the conversation on the phone the last couple of months about young Kelsey's situation to know their relationship. Bob's right of course. Kristian Mueller is in need of friendship as much as the rest of us, maybe more. I stop to introduce myself as I'm on my way to the Mens to relieve myself.

"Good of you to come out to pay your respects," I say.

"Yeah, well, it was the least—"

I know that look.

And then he almost loses it, blows his nose hard into a napkin, tips his head back and forward again, wipes his eyes with the back of his hands.

Lovesick. I decide to pull up a chair for a minute.

I nod to the corner of the bar where Daisy and Kelsey have the quilt bee going. "That your girl over there?"

He barely glances in Kelsey's direction. "She was, but I'm history now."

He's picking at some scabs on his arm.

"She sure is pretty."

"There's no way I can take care of her, let alone a baby."

I let that settle between us. Give him a pat on the back, and nod.

"It is a big responsibility, raising up another human being. There was a time when I was in a similar predicament, and in the dog house for it, so to speak."

He gives me a quick look.

"But my girl had the opposite problem. She couldn't have babies."

The young fellow stops picking at himself.

"Darned if I could figure that out. A young and healthy woman like Daisy, not that many years older than your Kelsey here at the time."

"She's not mine." He shakes his head vigourously side to side.

I ignore him.

"We went into the city, saw specialist after specialist, and got all the tests.

"For the longest time, I thought there must be something wrong with me because I'm a fair bit older than Daisy. That didn't make me feel very good. It also meant I wasn't much of a partner to her. Partnership, you know, that's one of the biggest things I've learned from marriage."

The young fellow screws up his face and starts to clear his throat and cough again and again, like he's got a big frog stuck down there.

"We kept trying and trying, but when it came to feeling the loss she was feeling, I wasn't much help to her. I kept thinking this problem will go away. Nope, didn't go away. Just made me feel worse about myself. And the losing was eating her up inside."

"I don't know." He's gasping for air.

"But here's the thing I've learned. Contrary to popular belief, women can be quite reasonable when given the chance. They'll usually tell you what they need if you listen.

"I kept thinking, that she kept thinking…

"Maybe it's not the way you think. Maybe the answer will come to you different than you expect."

The kid is shaking his head again. "Too late for that now."

"You see, in the end, she had to hear it from me. That she was okay and we were okay the two of us. That's all she needed.

"And I had to acknowledge the change it meant for her and let us both go through the process. Change, that's another thing I've learned at this game. It never stops."

"It's bigger than that."

"Always seems so when it's happening to us personally. Still, it sure is a blessing to have children. Hope you know that."

"Yeah." He takes a deep breath. "Sure."

There's always more than one way to skin a cat, Boy! I want to say. But instead, before I head back to the koffee klatch, I cuff him on the shoulder, just enough to maybe knock some sense into him.

8

MIKE

After the ladies start to serve sandwiches and Bob says he's not hungry, I ask him to hold the camera for a while. Something to keep him occupied. The truth is I'm hungry. I didn't get breakfast this morning. I was on the phone with Alex first thing, planning how we could move a few things up with the History Project, take advantage of the funeral on Saturday, and not wait for the decommissioning on Sunday. Now I grab a ham bun off the passing plate.

"You don't have to be a scientist to know," one of them is saying. "A little chem and a little biology."

"A lot of years on the ground."

"That's Agriculture Canada for you. Those guys with their university degrees, all theoretical, easy for them to say in their glassed-in atmosphere-controlled offices. 'We don't know yet if this is climate or weather.'"

"A winter like this last one."

"A spring with no moisture."

"The land is drying."

"Annie said as much."

We all pause and look in her direction as if on cue. Jack carefully wipes his eyes with his sleeve, then takes out his handkerchief and blows his nose.

"El Niño they call him and he is one hell of a current," Buster says after an appropriate pause.

"Big spreads of land, that's the way of the future," I say between bites. "Knock the fences down, drain all the sloughs. 'Efficiencies,' the banker explained it to me, the only way to survive. Maybe. Maybe for the younger ones coming up. Maybe for the banker. My kids have all left to the city, got educations, good jobs."

We take turns around the circle like it's the dead of winter or the height of summer and we're warming our hands over an open fire. I'm taking a mental sketch for a painting later; Annie's Wake I'll call it.

"It's a young man's game, farming." Buster shakes his head.

"The new machinery they've got, you need a ladder to get up the side of a tractor." Alex waves his battered cap like a flag in one hand and nurses a cup of coffee in the other.

"One man has to have the reach of five and the strength of twenty now they say." Buster squeezes his big hands and ripples his biceps ever so little as he says it.

"Wait for a foreign investor to buy your land and hire you as the manager." I take the last bite of my bun.

Bob looks like he's watching a tennis match, the camera bobbing from one side of the court to the other. Any minute now and he's going to provide commentary.

"They're not interested in land in this part of the province," Alex continues. "Well, maybe Victoire or Harmonie but not Majestic. Marginal grey soils, tree loam, a few inches of topsoil if you're lucky. Too much maintenance in the short term. Good for alfalfa. Oats or barley, better yields after hay or fallow. The big land companies don't have the patience. This country's a different kind of investment."

"You're not keeping up." I wink at Alex. "The big seed companies have crop rotation products for us too. GMOs. Kick-Ass Canola. Pretty soon, Kick-Ass Wheat. Kick-Ass everything. Decrease pests, increase yield. Everywhere comes up paradise."

The word "paradise" hovers in the air between us. Jack gets up and rearranges the roses in the vase at the foot of Annie's sheet-draped body, her hair all combed, her work shirt ironed. The bandanna around her neck looks almost festive. Still leaning on his cane, Jack moves the two taper candles ever so slightly away from the blooms. When he finds his seat again, we wait for him to lay down his cane. The top end of it hits the floor with a light clatter. Then we pick up the conversation again, right where we left off.

"How does that work?" Buster asks, taking a bite of his beef and horseradish sandwich.

"The first year, you put in oats. You spray a broadleaf herbicide the middle of May, just before seeding. The next year you use glyphosate and then plant the canola. The chemical kills all the volunteer oats and everything but the canola. The third year, you grow barley. You spray the soil before you plant with another herbicide mixed with glyphosate, to get rid of any residuals: weeds and last year's canola. Then hit it again just before harvest to dry the crop. Year four, you start the canola-go-round all over again.

"Skip the summer fallow. Plant the rows close. More yield, more production per acre that way. Better moisture retention. Less tillage. Less erosion. Less fuel. Less air pollution. Less herbicide in the end, they say."

Bob pulls back from the camera for a minute. "You know, they make some good points."

"Convenient that you have to buy the seed and the chemical from the same company though."

"They've got it all thought out."

"Sounds like something from *Star Trek*."

"I probably should have taken that university scholarship instead of agricultural college," I tell them.

"That's right, Mike, you could have been an engineer working in one of those corporations downtown by now, a head office maybe in utilities or chemicals or oil, though there's not too many of those left anymore." Alex settles back in his chair. "Heck, the dumbest of my high school classmates are managers, pulling down six-figure salaries."

"Yeah, blessed are the citified," Buster scoffs. "Spending their days driving this kid to ballet and that one to basketball. The next day it's Scouts and band. Hockey and bowling. No end to it."

"Buying flat screens for every room in the house," Alex takes up the chorus. "Renovating the bathroom every five years, matching towels and paint to the new tiles."

The circle starts to flex and crackle, like the conversation were a game. It's about the time when Annie would come around with refills, offer a retort, something pithy, that showed she'd listened too, and that for all her reticence, she was, to the rest of us, the smartest person in the room.

"It's true; I was bored to death," Jack speaks suddenly. "That was me for half the year when I wasn't in the field." His voice sounds distant, tired, and hollow. "I should have come back much sooner." He glances back at Annie when he says it. "After my wife died, I could have retired early." He let's one tear pass down his cheek, wipes it away. "Too many days spent pushing papers across a desk, looking out of highrise windows, wishing you could open them, to feel a breeze. I was boxed up in there so long I forgot what real weather felt like."

The room is silent for a few moments. It's as if the rest of us are breathing as one with Jack. From the kitchen, there's a nervous titter. A couple of our circle glance over at Annie to see how she's taking all this. A pall settles over the room, a deeper gloom.

"Now it's everywhere," Buster says. "This mad cow disease. Quicker than I thought." A new strand unspools in the circle of speech, new and somehow old too. Back to the very beginnings of just about everyone in the room. What would Annie say about survival?

Buster rearranges his hat on his knee. "With the border closed, the price has dropped to practically nothing. I took some head in last week and it hardly paid the shipping."

Alex takes a turn. "Here I was just trying to keep the bank at the door, praying for a change in the weather and now this. I've lost all of it — my initial investment, years of winter nights sleeping out in the barn pulling calves, a marriage, a son to the city. What I've got left: two hundred cows, this year's young, last year's steers."

Buster looks to each of us around the circle. "I might as well shoot the whole works. I'll never sell them. The auctions are rigged. The prices set in the States."

Alex nods. "If you want to sell, there's really only two companies. They set the price at head office. No negotiating."

"The meat's on the hood by eight o'clock in the morning and in the stockyards by nine." Buster pauses to frown. "They let it sit there a day or two, don't feed it."

"Let it drop some weight," Alex quips.

Jack nods. "Then they sell it."

"It's on a cattle liner to Calgary," Alex repeats what every one of us knows already, "butchered hanging on the hooks that same day. Everyone takes their piece of it along the way. The trucker, the stockyards, the railways, the meat companies, the grocery chains, the fast food franchises."

"Lucky if we get twenty cents a pound. Twenty months or forty months." Buster finishes his story: "It makes no difference. Butcher cows, twenty-five cents a pound. Three to four-hundred-pound steers, one-twenty-five a pound. It's been weeks now, the border closed."

"Weeks and no sign of let-up. That's what they say."

"Mad cow is here to stay."

"They don't even know what causes it. Not just contaminated feed."

"What they grow these days. Chickens that eat pig."

"Pigs that eat cows."

"Cows that eat each other."

"These critters can form on their own," Jack says. "In the brain from spontaneous mutations. Prions they call them."

"And where do they live before that," Buster wants to know. "In the liver? In the kidneys? I'm just thinking of cutting my losses."

"What would Annie have said?" Alex asks suddenly.

"Something contrary."

"The soil is your life."

"Treat the land like it is your own body." This last from Jack, who barely whispers the words, daubs his eyes quickly with the back of his hand, and looks straight ahead again.

"We're definitely too late for that the way this global warming is going," I say. And the circle starts to flex again.

"Soon we'll all be raising rabbits and selling like it was chicken."

"Just like the thirties."

"Worse. That's what Annie said. Drought year round. Winter and summer. No snow and no rain."

"Come to think of it, the snowshoe hares look to be the only creatures prospering through all this." Buster clears his throat.

"Like I said, I'm thinking of cutting my losses." He's turned serious all of a sudden. "I've got this idea to just let her go. The back quarter. Let her go back to the land. Let the poplar and the spruce and the birch retake her. Maybe keep the odd head of cattle, a cow for milking."

Jack looks up, looks hard at Buster.

"What are you talking about?" Alex says. "You can't just let it go to wild."

"Should never have been farmed. This is forest soil."

"What about your people?" Alex says.

"What about them? They're all gone."

"All that hardship, the years it took to pick the roots, burn the brush." Alex turns in his seat. "It was backbreaking. Without land where would we be?" Alex turns to the coffin at the head of our circle. "What if we could wind back the clock, reverse time?"

Then we hear it. Not out loud but in our minds, like an image, only in song. Annie's laughter. We all look at each other, then at our hands, startled.

Buster sticks his chin out of the silence. "All I know is that it can't continue this way."

"Why don't you sell then? Let someone else carry on?"

"Why, so they can fail too?"

"I don't know. Maybe."

"My grandparents made more per bushel than I am right now. With all the extra machinery costs, the amount of inputs: time, fertilizer, pesticides, seed. It all keeps going up. The outputs are only declining. That's what I know. I'd rather grow roses like Bob here. Don't need much for that. Cow manure, water, leaf mulch."

Bob sets the video camera down on his knee before he responds. "Buster's right. I'm going to clean out the old corral. Three feet of manure in there at least. Built-in fertilizer, properly aged." He looks around the circle. "I won't have to add nutrients or mulch for years.

I'm going to make it a microclimate, build a narrow shelter belt —
harder to do in a drought I know. Can't use any of the water-loving
trees."

"Now, I think you might have a situation of scents competing."
Buster sits back and smiles.

"No, this here would be an example of one scent transforming
another," Alex says.

"Alchemy, modern-style," Buster quips.

"Annie would approve," Jack's voice trembles.

Bob leans in, sets the camera on the floor in front of him, and
rubs his hands. "See, you can request just about anything on the
internet."

I can't help but laugh.

"All you have to do is sign up. I'm on the mail list for Kew
Gardens. They'll send seed just about anywhere. And all the horti-
cultural research stations. They're always coming up with new
varieties."

"Maybe you could open to the public, Bob."

"And we could all work for you in the summers when we've all
gone bust." Alex chortles and sits back in his chair.

The circle crackles again, pops. How to show this quality in
colours, in action? It's something I always puzzle over with the
Table of Truth.

"Rose gardens. They take a lot of water," I say.

"That's for sure," says Buster.

"And a lot of care," Jack chimes in, protection in his voice, still
glancing back at Annie.

Buster snorts. "Cripes, if those poor buggers in Cali can grow
commercial roses up the side of the bloody Andes, we can sure as
hell grow them here in Majestic."

"There's a market," someone else quips.

"Darn rights."

"This is not a commercial venture."

"We know, we know." Jack puts up his hand. "The fellows just can't resist pulling your leg, Bob. But we shouldn't. We should show our respect, seeing as this is a day for respects."

"Well, I appreciate your interest. I've researched it. The first three years are critical. They need watering, five gallons a week per bush. But once they're established their roots are like an auger to a well. They'll bloom fifteen to twenty years."

"Can't argue with that. Roses are nice. When I was in Ag at Olds, I used to help out in the greenhouse," I say, trying to smooth the feathers. "I liked working in the breeding section. All that crossing and mixing and splicing. Then waiting to see what happened."

Jack sits back in his chair again.

"I got my first shipment last week."

"Roses from Alberta." Jack shakes his head emphatically. "Annie would say, 'the toughest roses in the world.'"

Buster chins his way into the conversation again. "Remember that cemetery over at Reymund? That land was first cleared, what eighty years ago? It's been abandoned for forty years. Peaceful spot to walk on a summer's day. All going back to swamp. Overgrown with spruce, aspen, poplar, blue-eyed grass and wild rose, wood lily. The headstones, the fence posts, all of it under moss."

"Yup, I remember it, Buster," Jack says.

"Boreal forest that. Yup, once the native plants come back, the animals will too. Then I'll open it up like a natural game park. After the tour bus crowds are done seeing Bob's roses there, they can come by and pet the deer. Buy a few table linens too."

Bob takes up the camera again.

"I always knew you was an old hippie, Buster," Alex says.

"I've never known any hippies that trapped lynx for hide or

shot moose for meat." I point at Buster across the circle: "That's a mountain man.

"But, what's it all for?" I'm serious now. "All this science, this worrying about yields and technology? We're never going to make money. We make a lot of other people money: the equipment dealers, the fertilizer people, the pesticide industry."

"It's just so shady down there in that old cemetery," Buster says, poking his pipe deeper into his mouth, his other hand out of habit looking for matches he no longer carries in his chest pocket.

The conversation keeps turning back and back and back.

"But we're farmers." Alex is red in the face. "We have a responsibility to feed the world!"

That's when I decide to tell them. "Last week I took down all the breeding signs on the home place. The thoroughbred English Poll Hereford Angus Cross."

Buster doesn't skip a beat. "Let the world feed itself. I'm tired of subsidizing this city way of life. Let those people feed themselves. It's wrong-headed to think that we can feed everyone, that we're supposed to feed everyone. I'm not sure we're doing people any favours, feeding them."

"I'm cutting my herd in half," I add.

"My God, Buster, what about trade?" It's Alex again, ignoring me.

"What about it?"

"People have been trading since before the last ice age, for thousands of years before we got here. Speaking of roses!"

"Roses came from China over the Silk Road to Persia. And then to Europe. Annie told me that."

Jack barely nods his head. "Everything comes from Persia. Wheat, barley too. The fertile crescent."

"I've not given up on trade. Hudson's Bay still takes pelts. Just mail them off at the post office. Annie can attest to that."

There is a small pause in the proceedings, a nod in the direction of Annie, who even in death is still our hostess.

"What's Daisy think of all this?" Alex asks finally.

"The wife's got a good frontier clothing business going. Country Kitchen Linens: aprons, potholders, napkins, tablecloths, quilts. Has a mill in Mumbai she sources for the cotton. Everything's organic. Sells it all on the internet. I'll be damned if I can figure that world out. She's hired on that young Kelsey. Comes and helps her sew on the weekends. Lots of Americans looking to emulate life in the wild northwest. Quite lucrative."

I tease him, "You can be the house husband now," thinking, I already am one, between Vera's shifts and the girls gone.

"Darn rights. Have my friends over for coffee, watch the soaps. That woman's got more creativity than all the masters at the Louvre, I reckon. You should see the phone ringing, the pots boiling, sketches in every corner of the kitchen for this and that fabric. The woman's a veritable goldmine."

Alex persists, "But if we don't have grain, what? If we don't have beef?"

Buster is ignoring Alex's growing agitation. "I'm going to cut out California imports. Take the hundred-mile diet. Dig out the old root cellar, re-roof it. Grow my own carrots, potatoes, cabbage, and onions. They make a fine stew in winter."

It is Jack's turn to run philosophical. "Where did that start, this grand design to end famine? I wonder. When we got television on the farm? When we got radio? The year we got electricity?"

"Nineteen fifty-nine," I say.

"That started a hunger in us." Jack looks around the circle. People start to nod their heads. "Suddenly we were listening with our ears turned outward, the world was beaming in on us. News from all four corners. This disaster in Bangladesh, that famine in

Eritrea, the war in Biafra. Then television. Live feed in our small, modest living rooms, sitting on our worn couches. This hunger for more meaning. In the sixties, the call to feed the poor. That's when they started this push to modernize. Our animal manure was inferior. Our yields. We needed fertilizer. Pesticides. Herbicides. The Green Revolution. The grain company man and his promises. How we were going to feed the world!"

Buster shook his head. "It started the moment our grandfathers came across the ocean — newspaper advertisements and lantern shows — the idea of progress."

"Your people, Buster; yours too, Alex; mine; and Annie's." Jack shifts in his seat, looks her in the eye. "All of us leaving famine of some kind. That's how we got here."

"With threshing machines," I chime in. "And steam-powered tractors. Horse power without horses."

"Improvements sure to eliminate the uncertainties of living."

Alex has started to falter. "And here I am working longer and harder than my great-grandfather ever did, more in debt than he ever was. He had a big family, a wife and six kids. I bought the pesticides, I bought the fertilizer. I bought the horsepower. Now, I'm lucky if I can support myself on four times as much land."

"My great-grandfather warned my grandfather." Buster speaks up, "This won't come to no good. All this machinery, all this technology. People are excited by their own greatness. If a machine can do it, there's no more need of family, of community. It's a lonely life living with machines. A machine don't match a veritable human being."

"I've been farming some thirty years now and I seem to be feeding everyone but myself. The bank, the fertilizer companies, the seed corporations, the grain trade." The circle turns its gaze on me.

"I've been so busy feeding the planet, I haven't had the luxury of my own laying hens. All our milk comes from the store. Our vegetables. Even the old apple tree in the yard. Vera and I haven't had the time to pick it for years. We just let the fruit fall.

"That's how I came to painting."

Alex smiles at me from across the room. Bob's stops the camera. Buster jerks his head up so quickly he almost throws the coffee out of the mug in his hand.

Jack asks, "What have you been painting?"

"What it was like. You know, as a kid growing up, how bright everything seemed. The fair days. The gymkhana. The stores in town. The rail station. When we had passenger service twice a day." I can hear myself breathing fast. I clasp and unclasp my hands not sure where to put them suddenly.

"I think Annie knew from the parcels. She winked at me one day after the first dozen deliveries or so. 'Looks like you have your own rose project going there, Mike.'"

"How long?" Jack asks now.

"Two winters. I go out to my barn early after Vera is off to the hospital and after I feed the cattle. I hole myself up for the day."

"Now, isn't that something," Buster says.

"During summers I take photographs or make sketches."

Just then Father Pat interrupts the group. He's only just arrived and Buster whispers in Bob's ear, "Remember the History Project?

"Change of plans, boy. *Carpe diem.*" Buster winks. "Watch me; watch the padre."

"Yes, that History Project has had a change of schedule," Jack says loudly. Heads nod. Even the priest looks pleased to hear the word "history" and smiles in the group's direction. "Everything moves up a couple of days," Jack says in a normal voice, and then more quietly, "Negotiations start tonight."

BUSTER

The truth is I'd be visiting the Emerg if it weren't for Daisy. I'm a total fumble fingers when it comes to making things, cloth or otherwise, (animals are my thing), but if I could wield a pair of scissors I'd be down in the basement helping her. As it is I try to help out in other ways, but she's the only reason right now that our enterprise is staying afloat. We have another income stream, and I can write my losses off against her gains.

I'm only half-joking when I talk about a game park. Not one with pens or cages. I wouldn't bother with fences either. Put out a few bales of hay in the winter, sew the cultivated parts to wild grasses and then leave it.

Unlike Alex, I just want to sit on my horse, so to speak, and live out the rest of my days in peace. Running cattle worked well enough while it lasted, but times change and like they say, you have to adapt or die. Now, if only I can talk Daisy into it. Shouldn't be too hard. Hah! It does give me a chuckle to see Alex screw up his face when I tease. That guy's got to lighten up or he's gonna die premature.

ALEX

I have to admit I could use a rose or two in my life and by that I mean some female companionship. Annie hinted as much when she was alive. Saved the Personals for me from the weekend paper. Put them in my mailbox.

I've been living too much in my own head these past few years. I told Buster this past winter, I'm starting to talk to the calves.

"Watch yourself! Next you'll be having relations of an unnatural kind."

Sometimes I have Sunday supper with him and Daisy. Sometimes it's Mike and Vera.

"But who's a match around here?" I ask them.

Buster says, at these auction sales I attend, I should hang out at the food stations, chat up the servers. Get second and third cups of coffee.

"Cripes, I'll be spending all my time in the toilets that way."

Daisy says I should get on the internet, find a widow, someone who likes the rural life, grew up with it or was married to it. "Farm life requires a woman with a certain amount of independence." She's probably right.

Buster teases. "Yup, even at forty-eight you've still got some life left in you."

Both of them say I should come out to community dances again, even if there's no one here in Majestic I want to settle down with. Women all like to dance. "Besides, you're rusty." Buster arches his brow at me, old cagey eyes. "You'll need it if you want to go courting again."

Daisy says something similar. "Maybe sign up for one of those cooking classes in Victoire in winter. It would get you out. Plus lots of women go to those classes. If nothing else you'll learn how to make a couple of dishes. Women these days expect their husbands to be able to cook something, you know."

That's when Buster laughs.

"Even if it's only breakfast," she adds. "But aside from that, you'll eat better. Buster starts supper for me all the time." She smiles over the table at him. "Sometimes, if I've got a lot of orders to get out, like at Christmas, Buster'll just say, 'What's on the menu?' and do the whole show. He can peel potatoes as good as I can."

Buster winks at me. "Darn'd if she isn't giving away all the secrets of her fair sex."

I don't tell anyone that Annie was the only one I ever spoke to about my divorce. I would go to town the middle of the afternoon, every other week, no one else around, and she would pour me coffee and say, "How you doing, Alex?" And we would go from there.

9

FLORENCE

The good father looks startled when he arrives at the wake early Friday evening. He says nothing at first. There is a crowd packed into this old public house: everyone whom Annie has ever helped, whom her grandmother had ever healed. Afflictions, blights, tangled births, droughts, poor crops. There is talk of capturing her likeness, making a memorial card of her face, of the special wounds on her neck. A small group of women in the corner are praying the rosary. In another corner, people are taking turns with the scissors and the iron, cutting strips of pattern and colour. Daisy is urging them on, saying "The brighter the better." Some are stitching with Daisy, old-fashioned-like, by hand, satin stitches. It's a crazy quilt. Kelsey is making a magpie for the centre block, from solid black and white and polka dot scraps. Just like a magpie to be surrounded by shiny things, I think. The young Mueller boy, Kristian, is still sitting in the same corner off by himself, his shoulders hunched now, head in hands, rocking back and forth. Daisy says it's a good sign that he's here, that maybe he wants to mend things, but the young miss is pretty much ignoring him. And I can't blame her.

"Mike," says one of the old men, "are you getting this down?" Mike has brought his video camera. He's recording the whole thing. Sandwiches and squares are being passed around. Egg salad and tuna fish. Nanaimo bars and date squares.

I glance back at Annie laid out on the table, and I give a little start. Father Pat has put down his case near her and opened it, rummaging for something inside. And I swear can see her trying to rise and hear her in my mind wanting to pray her own service.

FATHER PAT

They are all talking farming when I get to there to do the vigil service. Roses and crops and drought. Beef prices depressed and pork futures down. The money they owe the banks, the mortgages on their land. The weather.

Someone has put a yellow and orange banner over the dart board: Sing Hallelujah! Someone else is videotaping the whole carnival. The body has been on display all day. Lucky it isn't hot outside, but they've got the air conditioner going in here too. No smell yet. Florence has roses set around the room, sticks of incense burning on some windowsills. Daisy is just setting out fresh candles by Annie's head and her feet and is about to light them.

I put down my carrying case, take out more votive candles, ask the women to put them around the place. Pull out my crucifix, set it at the head of the body.

I throw my prayer stole over my black cassock, turn around, measure the two ends, make sure they fall even, turn back to the room. Take out my book of funeral rites, turn to the section on Funeral Vigils or wakes as they are traditionally called. That's when I interrupt the visiting, tell them it's in poor taste.

"But father, we're doing what we always do around Annie."

"Just like old times."

"Mornings at the post office."

"Annie would put on the coffee," one of the old codgers assures me. "We'd get the mail, shoot the breeze."

"She'd sit in her wicket there and listen. She could talk farming as good as any of us."

It's well past coffee time I remind them. They seem surprised. I gather some of them have been at it all day and haven't noticed the time passing. I ask everyone to clear the space around her, allow people to approach with their last respects. They pile the small round tables against the wall and start to arrange the chairs in a series of concentric circles, till it looks like any other public space, except for the cabinet behind the bar with liquor stacked to the ceiling. The hotel is all finished inside in the style of the thirties. The bar itself is solid mahogany, probably made from a single tree, the grain lines up so well. Between here and the church, this is the fairer building by far. It's easy to see that.

The people start a procession to view the body. At least a hundred people, more than actually live in the town. The line keeps growing. I recognize some of the faces from the parish, but many not.

KRISTIAN

I see the tone of the light before I see the body laid out on a table. I hesitate at first, but then I decide to walk up to it just like everyone else, pretend I see like everyone else.

She is smiling. There are no tire tracks on her face. I have to hold myself back from getting closer, from touching her; something makes me want to touch the field of light around her. I keep holding myself a little distant from the foot of the table, squeezing my arms around myself I realize, trying to stop them from shaking.

"But I saw her face—" I start to say to the lady by the coffin and she grabs her gut like I've just punched her. I want to say, I saw her face go under, she was smiling, just like she is here.

Instead I ask, "Did they change how she looked or did she come in this way?" doubting again.

The lady studies me for a minute, kind of puzzled and nutty-looking, like she's off somewhere in her head, and I had woken her.

"No, Krisitan. I helped with the body." That's when she gives a little whimper and I recognize her – Miss Florence from Grade 1.

"She was like that when she was found; we didn't use any make-up on her."

"Thanks," I say, "I'm really sorry for my questions." I untwist my arms, stuff my hands in my pant pockets, and start to back away.

People are splashing themselves, crossing themselves with water that was set out in a bowl at the foot of the table where they've laid her. I just follow along and cross myself too. I turn back to get one last look. That's when I think I see her peeking over the edge of her casket, smiling. I think, it must be a trick of the light, all of it, then and now. Somehow her body got twisted and if I could see the back of her, I'd find the tire tracks, the evidence. The sun is coming in hard through the back window. Yes, a trick of the light.

I start to get choked up again and this big old gruff guy with a gimped leg, gives me a slap on the back, and says she was one of the good ones and it was too bad. The greater the gift the greater the loss. The greater the love ... and a few other things. I keep wiping the tears from my eyes.

Finally the line snakes back to where it began, and half the participants find seats, while the other half, mostly the men, remain standing. Time to start.

"My dear people, I welcome you to this vigil for our friend and neighbour, Anna Marie Gallagher." Conversation stops, chairs shuffle and scrape.

Mrs. Cummins plays the piano in the corner. I'm sure it hasn't been tuned in decades. She and Florence lead the congregation in a very slow rendition of *Holy Holy Holy*. One verse.

Lord God Almighty. Indeed.

Early in the morning our song shall rise to Thee.

Early in the evening perhaps…. At least nobody needs to look at the hymnbooks. They all know it. Second verse.

"My dear people—" I start, but I'm cut off. Mrs. Cummins frowns, bends towards Florence, bends towards the piano, third verse.

Holy, holy, holy! All the saints adore Thee.

Really now, this is a bit much. We never sing the third verse for the opening unless it's Christmas!

Mrs. Cummins takes her hands off the piano when she sees me glaring, and she and the congregation comes to a jagged halt on the last note of the last verse: *be Be BE bee beez.*

"My dear people, let us pray for the repose of the soul of Anna Marie Gallagher. Heavenly Father we ask for your gentle light to shine on our sister. We pray that you will greet her with open arms and take her home to you."

Florence and Vera and Daisy chorus "Amen." Everyone else nods. It's like Catholics forget what to bloody do when they've got Protestants in the room.

Florence Enders gets up to do the first reading.

But the souls of the just are in the hand of God, and no torment shall touch them.

Yes, there is always a "but" with God.

ANNIE

No torment shall reach me here. My affliction is over. I am worthy. Proved like gold. Proved in a fire hotter than the kiln I grew up with.

My tears have been my food day and night.

So they have. So they have.

Touch has been my suffering and my redemption. Nothing more to touch, no more to be touched in this body.

After the institution, after the city, when I came home again to my father's house, I saw his thick hands as if for the first time, muscled, scarred, so many tiny flecks of white skin where the coals had sent up sparks and burned through. Some, where skin had grown over, where it was jagged, ruptured. I saw his bloated face, his veined nose, his handkerchiefs filled with black from the kilns even though he hadn't worked them for years.

Kristian sees the air above him white as light through a fog. Sees the aura of peace on the ceiling. Doesn't know what it is. But your heart calms, doesn't it? From here on the ceiling I can see you grip the seat, look up, listen.

They seemed, in view of the foolish, to be dead; and their passing away was thought an affliction and their going forth from us, utter destruction. But they are at peace.

Is it true what they say about the dead? Kristian's thinking. *That their eyes can see through mass? That they can see into your very soul?*

A wonder he can't hear me laughing.

As gold in the furnace, he proved them, and as sacrificial offerings he took them to himself. Someone is saying.

Bob is weeping, covering his eyes, his head down on his knees. Vera is comforting him, patting him on the back.

In the time of their visitation, they shall shine, and shall dart about as sparks through stubble. So they will.

Dear Bob, now I'll always be present in your roses, the light in the stubble. I'll always be where I fell, where they marked the well. I didn't have to count. Sixty feet deep, twenty-five gallons per minute. Not deep at all in these times. A blessed aquifer you're living on top of there.

"Annie," he whispers, down on his knees, rubbing his ears then his eyes, weeping. He dries himself carefully with a sleeve. "Truly?"

Truly I tell you, as the sparks run through the field, as on the day of visitation. Go back and check for yourself. The place where I put all the little flags, around the body, where the lightning burned the ground. Drill. It's no wonder I got hit — so much water there.

He's crossing himself now, "Holy Mother of God. It's a miracle," he's saying to anyone who will listen. But no one is paying attention yet. They have their own mortality to come to terms with first. No miracles in that.

Buster is behind him, wrinkling his brow, thinking how Bob appears to be talking to himself.

It's funny what you can see from this vantage point.

As a deer longs for streams of water, so my soul longs... What is your name? When shall I see your face? When shall I see the face of God? All my life I've wandered roads, fields, rivers looking for you. In the moment of the finding, overcome.

Deep calls to deep... In the roar of your torrents all your waves and breakers sweep over me. All the oceans, the rivers, the streams, underground tributaries run through me. As long as there is water. That is your promise.

Awake, O Sleeper...

Wake, Oh wake, sleeper, wake from thy slumber wake! Wake, wake me, stay awake, wake the dead. Sprinkle water, make a blessing, like a children's game. The magpies keeping vigil. I saw them too, *caw caw* a hundred-thousand times the chorus. To be loved like that. That's all I've ever wanted. To fill the ache in me. The roar of fellow creatures, the highest compliment. My passing noted in the hearts of birds. Who says they have no heart-brains? We are not far from each other in nature's terms. Only our thoughts need to turn towards them.

I have gone nowhere I have not been before. Mine has been a life of living between the worlds. The artist sees, the sage knows, the saint prays. Mike, Jack, Florence. Close to death, close to life. It's the way we come at things, slanted, a sidelong glance. Never approach the source of water directly, circle round, and come at an angle, a side-stepping journey. Where Florence goes with the rosary, where the paints take Mike, the stories, Jack. How I find the water.

Creatures are naturally shy of their talent, like the young Kristian frightened by his own gift. *Come Holy Spirit.* Yes, come. The priest is young. He sees the least: less than the boy, less than the girl, Kelsey. He does not yet know the terrible holy. He does not begin to know true evil or true good.

I say to you, unless a grain of wheat falls to the ground and dies, it remains just a grain of wheat; but if it dies, it produces much fruit.

ALEX

I don't say this now, but a person needs their experience, the good and the bad. Needs a clarity of where they're going. And other people for shade and mutual nurturance. There is sacrifice and losing oneself. It's always a risk. There are never any guarantees of harvest, but whatever you put your faith in, it has to quench your thirst, it has to warm you inside. There's a certain stillness in the process. Even for me, I realize, it can't only be about the farming. Busy won't erase the loss.

I make a point of standing up to speak, my hat in hand.

"There are at least three omissions in that gospel. There needs to be death in the soil too — soil needs dead plant matter. Death feeds the soil. There needs to be light and there needs to be water. All three. Death, water, light. Everyone knows, without the three, the grain won't germinate.

"Annie was the death and the water and the light."

As I settle back into my seat I glance over at the young priest. His eyes narrow, his cheeks puff up. Too late, I want to tell him. You're no match for the salt of the earth.

ANNIE

The birds were an omen that spring twenty-eight years ago. Waxwings flinging themselves against the large picture window, drunk on fermenting mountain ash berries still clustered on the trees out front, driving themselves hard against the windows, like bully boys out on a night's spree. Maybe that's why they call them bohemian. Or maybe it's their dress, their bold colours.

They kept coming even when I rushed outside with a red dishtowel, the only thing I could find quick, wakened out of my own dozy wine-drugged sleep. I tried to warn them away. Spring was late in coming, the snow was still crusty and deep, and they were starving.

Afterwards I stood vigil over the little bodies, those that had crashed their wings, broken their necks, keeping the magpies at bay. A half dozen of the brightly painted folk, languishing, putting up a show of survival, pushing their chests out, slowly spreading their wings, their eyes half-closed, their breathing laboured, their heads sunk low and lower on their chests till they nodded off.

I saw myself in that moment as I had been for many years — trying to fill myself with things that didn't feed, flinging myself against unnatural structures in my own mind — hate and fear — not being able to stop myself. It was my own life I was seeing before me. I had no base from which to speak to the birds. I could not warn them from something I was doing to myself.

I buried every one. Picked up their cold feathered bundles carefully in my warm hands, laid them down at the foot of one of the apple trees in the backyard where my nana used to bury afterbirths of the women she helped to labour. Dug a hole in the hard earth and made a place for each of them, a bed to rest. Said a prayer over the graves and swore to Our Lady I would stop drinking if she let me live out my last days in peace. I chose to confide in Vera. She was different. I could see that. She never was one to run with the other children. She was always off by herself, thinking, watching. If someone fell on the playground she stopped to check on them. She wasn't one to force herself. She would just say, "Are you all right?" And with me, unlike some in town, she was never afraid.

I visited Florence too when I sobered up. Called at her house, unannounced. When she opened the door, she was shocked to see me. We hadn't spoken for so long. "Let's let bygones be bygones," I managed to say to her. "Please, could you pray for me?" So Vera nursed me and Florence fed me prayers and casseroles.

VERA

People begin to rise, to speak. The sun is low in the sky, only the candlelight to see by. It's as if the darkness were a mirror of all that we feel inside. A curtain to hide behind, a veil for refuge and a confessional. A teenage boy is weeping just back from the circle that's formed around the bier. But he is not the only one. My Mike has a tear. Alex.

DAISY

"Most of you know that I've never been able to have children. I've had so many miscarriages. Annie understood women's problems. She had them too. So how was it that she stayed so strong?

"I think she communicated with the water. Though I wasn't ever sure how.

"When her grandmother died, that kerfuffle happened and Annie was sent away. When she first came back, people kept clear of her and her father — they didn't want to be tarnished with town gossip. Till we needed a new well and my father remembering her grandmother, asked Annie if she could help. She used willow branches and walked in a trance around and round and the well continues to pump on that farm. After that, everyone started calling her, even when she was still drinking.

"I went to her too, after I was married, hoping for a cure. All I'd ever wanted was to be a mother. Annie gave me a bit of advice. 'Daisy there are some things you cannot mend, but you can mend yourself.' She was good that way with people. She could find just the right word to make you think. 'You need a purpose of your own,' she said to me, 'even if you could have children. Why not live and see what happens?'

"And that's where I got the idea for my business, and I went home and told Buster and he said it sounded like the best thing since apple pie.

"'I want to make things with my hands that will help other people make homes,' I told him. We really talked then, for the first time in months.

"And that's when he told me, 'Daisy, I married you for you, not for how many children you can have.'"

But before I can properly finish the story, I start to bawl. Then again, I suppose everyone in that room already knows how happy Buster and I are together.

VERA

"I still remember one late winter day, Annie came to my parents' house. We used to live the next block over from the old Gallagher place, where Annie took up residence when she came back to Majestic from the institution and after her father had died. I'd just finished my nursing degree and was going on to get my nurse practitioner certificate to go work up north. I'd done one of my rotations at a drug and alcohol treatment centre. My dad was always talking about me down at the hotel and what I was up to.

"She was starting to have blood come up, like her father had before he died. Blood in her stools, blood in her cough. But there was something else. 'A sign,' she called it. 'I've had a sign.' She had lost feeling in her hands, her witching arms. 'I know what I have to do. Will you stay with me while I go through it?'

"First she walked me to all her stashes in the house and we poured them out.

"I stayed with her for three weeks. My dad ran the bar for her while she dried out.

"Alcohol affects women differently than men — the damage is quicker, harsher. Annie had lost function in one kidney. She had stomach ulcers. I had to hold her and she needed medication, she was shaking so much from the withdrawal. She had nightmares remembering the institution she was in as a child. The locked doors, the restraints, the surgery they made her have.

"She'd dreamed of her grandmother during that time telling her what she had to do to heal. That she had to cry all the grief out of her or she'd die. Even the grief that she could never have children. They had cut that part out of her at the institution.

"But there is more. I owe Annie my calling. She told me I was a midwife just like her grandmother, of souls. Annie made me realize I could work with people in crisis, that it is a privilege and a gift to work with people when they are at a crossroads. That change is the most potent magic. Some people it sets off; I thrive on it."

I can't say anymore after that. I have to sit down, and when I do, I find Mike's arm is around me.

KELSEY

First thing, I look them straight in the eye, the way Miss Annie taught me. *Hold up your head; you have nothing to be ashamed of.* Sweeping my eyes around the room, even at Kristian, though he ducks when I glance his way. And then I speak.

"It was late April and still chilly at nights. Sometime in the early morning, Miss Annie said she'd felt something wasn't right in the ground at her place and she'd been driven out to check the four boundaries. That's what she called it. One of her cats had alerted her. I think she had x-ray vision. She just knew where to look. She came straight for me and she found me shivering and my teeth rattling where I was hiding under the caragana hedge.

I told her everything that had happened and how mad my mom was with me. And she said, 'Don't worry, come in for the night. It's cold out here.'

"She brought me inside into her kitchen and gave me hot chocolate and set up a bed for me with a crazy quilt in a bedroom she called the birthing room. I hardly knew Miss Annie before that night. She was just that funny-looking lady who lived next door and wore old coveralls and flannel shirts and a cowboy hat that looked oiled. She had a lot of cats that would come and go, and she would put food out for them in her backyard. Sometimes the Fire Department had to be called to rescue one of them off her roof. My mom said she was a witch of some kind, and that I shouldn't talk to her. Sometimes I saw her out working in her garden and she used to make a point of straightening herself and saying Good morning and Nice weather, but I would never say boo.

"The next day she said, 'You can stay with me as long as you like, but you have to go to school or get a job. Your mother's right. There are no free rides. Everyone has to do their part.'

"She was the one that made me think about church too. It was nothing she said. I just asked if I could come along. She hesitated a minute and then she grinned. 'It might be good for the baby. Churches like babies,' she said.

"I'd had my first communion when I was a little kid and Miss Florence said that's all I needed to be an altar server, that it would build heart in me. And that's what I needed to be a mom."

JACK

Between the tissue box and Florence standing by her, the young woman is pretty emotional. When she gets to the end, she almost breaks: "I just want to say that Miss Annie — saved my life. And I don't know where I'd be without her. I mean, I was like that reading, lost. I would never have turned it around."

Then she has to stop to wipe away her tears.

That young Mueller at the back of the bar looks like a jack-in-the-box, popping his head up and down all the way through, taking in every word the girl has to say. One minute sitting, one minute standing, looking up at the proceedings, then down at his feet.

When I get up to speak, I take my cue from the girl: "Yes, I imagine Annie's saved a lot of us around this room." And I see that young boy jump to attention.

"Years ago I fancied Annie. After she came back and before her father died. She was a beautiful thing, it was like the wild coursed through her. I knew she was dangerous too, so much power in one body. I sought her out. I would go to the bar just to catch a glimpse of her, to hear the roughness of her voice.

"My parents caught wind of it and forbade me to see her. 'That family's cursed. The mother abandoning her like that and not right in the head. Her father, a drinker.' According to them, nothing good had ever come from that home. My parents never spoke of the healing, the wells that were witched, the troubles mended, the bricks that built houses in these parts after the Great War, even our house.

"It was Annie's power and her grandmother's power, the power of the earth that made me want to study geology. So I lived between city and wilderness for thirty-odd years. I spent six months of the year in the field, chipping rock, drilling core samples, wandering mountain trails, forest floors, cutlines, and road allowances. Watching and listening. Having a family, a loving wife, and a good life. My wife has passed on, my children are grown and happy now, and I have no regrets. But I often wonder what would have come of it if I had defied my parents. I'm not ashamed to say that now I'm an old man, I know we're capable of loving many people in a lifetime.

"People would ask her to witch for them but she wouldn't accept any money, just like her grandmother. 'It's a gift,' she'd say. Only a gift could be given in return, and nothing that would cause hardship. But in the early years a bottle of whisky wouldn't be turned away."

The room laughs.

"She also accepted food as her grandmother had: eggs, milk, chickens, a cut of beef.

"After my wife died and I had moved back here, I visited her often. Once when we were alone, I asked her, would she marry me? 'No Jack,' she said, 'I was never meant to marry anyone. But you may love me if you wish.' And so I did.

"I used to have a ring of silver, a common enough ring in my profession. There are crossed pickaxes on it. I asked Annie if she would wear it for me, for the divining. She said 'Yes,' and she did. That was enough."

At the end of my speech, it is all I can do to find my seat again, even though I am standing right over it. The young girl hands me the box of tissues. It is my turn for tears.

FLORENCE

The good Father is scandalized by Jack's declaration. "This is an abomination!" he whispers in my ear and starts to rise to put a stop to the whole proceeding. I put out my arm to stop him, get up instead myself to speak.

"We were estranged, Annie and I, for so many years. When she came back to the church, she refused communion. Out of respect for me. When I was very young, I had an abortion."

Some ladies gasp, some men clear their throats, check the

positions of their chairs, scrape the floorboards as they shift a quarter of an inch. I feel my eyes starting to fill, but I will myself to stand taller, not to cry.

"Annie was a witness, though I don't think she understood the full import of what was happening that day. We were both very young."

Someone lets out an involuntary "Ah!" that ripples in the evening air, the release of innocence and sorrow.

The good Father starts to rise again; I stop him again.

"Not to worry, Father, I have long repented of my part, the child who had a child who she couldn't bear with the countenance of her father.... Dozens of priests have tried to absolve me; but only now have I been able to forgive myself. What I want to say today is that she is present in the water."

The good father rises abruptly and with both hands on my shoulders, feigns to help me find my seat, gives a curt nod to Kelsey, who opens the book upon cue, whereupon he starts to pray for peace in the world, for all those who have died, for all those who had gathered to worship and for Annie, that God might free her from punishment and darkness and forgive all her sins. And we all cant, "Hear us, Lord, and have mercy." The priest blesses us in the name of the Trinity, making the sign of the cross in the air over our bent heads. We take our collective revenge in the singing. Singing louder and longer, all three verses, making him wait.

Immaculate Mary, your praises we sing;
You reign now in heaven with Jesus our King.
Ave, ave, ave Maria,
Ave, ave, ave Maria.

Hail Mary. Only afterwards do I notice my wet cheeks. Again, the blessed water. I let them fall, let others fuss to uncover the dessert squares we've been saving to the end, break out the lemonade behind the bar. Pass out the coffee, and yes, the spirits.

Seventeen years old, a petty thief, meth head, liar, about-to-be dead-beat dad and now, murderer. Old enough to go to adult court. Old enough to get Life. This is what I've come to.

"You're in with a bad crowd," my old man said last winter, and I mimicked his bad English to his face: "Bad crowd, huh?" What an understatement. I mean look what I've done. This old guy who loved Miss Annie, and it was so hard to love her, and they were parted for so long, and they finally got together and he was her one true love. All these friends of hers and she had such a hard life and she finally got all her shit together and I come along and royally screw it up again, don't I? Like I screw up everything and every-one around me? I mean there's no coming back from death. That's it. I know. My mom died. The Old Man and I, we just look at each other most days. We don't know what to say. We sit across from each other at the table and eat the roast beef or the pork chops or whatever it is he's cooked for us that tastes like the insides of an old rubber tire. I know he cries himself to sleep at night. I do too. It's like we quit being a family when she died. Quit going to sports days, to church suppers, to town.

Why can't I just be normal? Why can't I have a head like every-one else's? Why did my mom have to die and leave the Old Man and me all by ourselves? My ma knew about my seeing. She saw the same way. She explained things to me, what it all meant. She made me feel normal. I felt good in my own skin. Like Kelsey. God, I miss her. And I don't deserve her.

The last hymn has hardly been sung when they arrive through the lobby of the hotel. There are three of them, hair in weird combinations of slicked and shaved, muscle shirts and tattoos up and down their arms and on their cheeks. At least one has a St. Christopher's medal around his neck. He seems to be the leader. When he sees the priest and the coffin and the packed-in crowd, he hesitates. Then he spots Kristian, who still has his head in his hands, sitting on a chair in a far corner, rocking himself.

I poke Bob in the ribs, who looks at me, looks where my eyes direct him, turns his camera on the Musketeers and starts to film. By then Alex sees them too and signals to Buster. Jack rises and looks around, one arm leaning on Annie's table, his cane ready to move. The five of us, by unspoken agreement, converge from our difference corners, stop a few feet short of the threshold and form a kind of wall. Buster greets their leader, the guy with the medal.

"What would you be looking for, young fellow? You're not a Gallagher are you?"

Buster is being polite; we've seen a couple of them driving around town before.

One of them tries to cover his face from the camera. The leader keeps a steady stare as he speaks, "Stand aside Old Man. We just want to talk to that dude in the corner," and flicks his head in the direction of Kristian. Kristian can't hear them for the din in the room.

The five of us move over to block their view. We take a small step towards them and then another, like a shuffle, until Buster is towering over the lead kid.

"I'm not as old as you might think," Buster drawls. "Besides, I'm pretty sure we outnumber you."

One of the kids starts to laugh until Bob zooms the camera in on him. "Hey! Stop that. There's such a thing as privacy rights!"

"Not in a public house," Buster quips.

The kid hiding his face takes a step back and his friends with him. We take another step towards them and nearly have them backed into the mail counter.

"Awful bad luck to harm anyone who's bereaved," Buster continues. "Especially when the reason for their sorrowing might find its way back to you."

I look out the window; it's still light. Take out the blank notebook I keep in my shirt pocket and write out the make and model of the dark SUV sitting there on an angle in the middle of the lane right where they left it. "END 223." I say aloud. Their licence number.

"Hey," the young fellow says. "We're not doing nothing wrong."

"Hey," Buster says in a quiet voice, "you're disturbing the peace and trespassing."

Just then Father Pat comes over, still in his black robes, and the young fellow with the medal freezes.

"What is the meaning of this?"

"Some of the local outlaws," Alex says.

"Let's get outta here," St. Christopher says to his buddies.

But we don't leave it there. We follow them out, six of us now, a couple of us crippled but all of us tough birds, filming them all the way to their car and even as they make a "u-ey" and head back to the highway.

10

BUSTER

After the wake proper is over, and the intruders have been suitably dispatched, Bob and I are waiting for the young priest by the tea station. The man is a tea drinker still in this day and age. I say, "Here he comes," poking Bob in the ribs. "Now's your chance."

His cup's full and he's loaded up on some of Daisy's baking.

I thrust out my right hand, pull Bob along by the shoulder.

"Father Pat, you remember me — from church suppers and graveyard cleanup days and the like. I'm with the Majestic ecumenical committee. United Church."

The priest nods but keeps his distance.

"This here is Bob Taylor. He's new to these parts, but he's expressed some interest in the real estate you've got on offer. I said I'd introduce you."

Bob steps forward, offers his hand. "Nice to meet you, Father."

Father Pat gives him a once over while they shake hands. Has he seen him before? Best to push on.

"Bob's a carpenter by trade. Thinking of repurposing the church into condos for city people maybe. Mind you, I told him, no citified folk are going to want to live next door to that old hotel or in the middle of this godforsaken — Oh excuse me, Father — this forgotten outpost. All these farmers and roughnecks and tool pushers and land men — it's all oil and gas around here, your Reverend. Oil and seismic and farming, but the farming hasn't been so prosperous these last few years. Enough to make people lose faith. But like I was saying, he can't be talked out of it. Maybe that's 'cause he's a city person himself and an atheist."

"An atheist?" Bob looks offended.

"Well, you don't belong to any church, right?"

"Well, that's true—"

"Fallen in love with the romance of living in the country, haven't ye." I poke him in the ribs. He clears his throat.

"Well, that's true," he says, all agreeable-like now. "I think I could really facilitate things here," Bob says, giving the priest a meaningful look. "You see, I want to renovate the place, turn it into a set of lofts. Call it 'country living close to the city.' A lot of commuters around here, Father. You know we're only an hour from the city on stormy days, forty minutes on good days. A paved road through town that runs all the way to the main highway. Can't beat it. The high ceiling will give the lofts character. The stained glass. That foundation, a yard thick, will last forever. The place is fully insulated. Well, you saw to that."

The priest stretches his neck, practically starts to preen himself. I give Bob a nod of appreciation. Flattery is the best card to play in the presence of the petty powerful.

"And you're not religious?" Father Pat asks.

"Not at all."

The priest takes a sip from his teacup. Sets it back in the saucer. I look for a flag in the pinkie finger. Sure enough. "You're very familiar with the property, Mr. Taylor."

"No more familiar than anyone else who knows the business and lives in a small town." Bob folds his arms.

Yeah, we never miss a trick, I was about to add, but thought better of it. Instead I take the Father's side. "R-400 insulation. Latest energy-efficient furnace."

The priest's Adam's apple is dancing like a water pump, his fine hand squeezing the big cross that hangs from his neck. I can see we are having the desired effect.

Bob keeps playing his cards. "The windows are an extravagance and a liability with gas bills, but they add interest. City folks are always looking for enticements. Some might like the idea of ghosts afoot."

Father Pat ignores the reference to haunting. There's never been any rumours about ghosts in that church. Mind you, it's never been abandoned before.

"What do you think the property is worth, Mr. Taylor?"

"Hard to say," replies Bob, evading the question. "The land is not worth that much."

Everyone knows that the first person to set the price is the one at a disadvantage. Always better to counter-offer. I step forward. "What are you asking for it, Father?"

"Well." The priest looks around first to see if we might be overheard, fidgets with his teacup. "Five thousand."

"Five thousand!"

The padre waves his free hand in front of me, as if to say, keep it down.

"Five thousand?" I manage a hoarse whisper. "Well I doubt it's worth half that when you consider it's up on the hill here, exposed to the elements, surrounded by the descendants of bushwhackers and railroad men. Five thousand sounds like a prosperous town down the track a ways. Besides, it looks to me like it needs a new roof."

I nudged Bob here who nodded his head on cue.

"We had this church — this property," the priest corrects himself, "appraised by the realtor in Victoire. They put it close to five thousand. The building — and the land."

"Five thousand seems high," Bob repeats, "especially when most lots in this town go for five hundred. You can get a grave for fifty bucks. Ground ain't worth much around here."

Bob is doing his best farmer talk. He's doing all right.

"And the building needs some serious upgrades."

Always unnerves the padres, farmer talk.

"But you say yourself, city people, they won't know the difference. They'll pay big prices."

"Or not. It's a risk." Bob lowers his voice, makes a point of staring over in the general vicinity of Florence Enders. "Like Buster says, will they want to live next door to roughnecks and landmen and seismic crews and unbalanced women?"

"And children," I finish. "You saw a few of them earlier tonight. Unruly types."

At this last, the priest winces.

"Mostly Catholic, I might add. The lapsed variety. Kind of like Jack Mormons. Gone wild."

At which the padre screws up his mouth and puts the padlock on.

"It's also next door to the hotel. Not a pretty picture on a Saturday night. Majestic bar where the drilling crews, the farmers, the Hutterites, and the Cree Nation meet."

The priest clears his throat. Takes another sip of his tea, his pinky finger rising. "So I've heard."

"Old Father Macdonnell used to say it was the most fertile place to save souls. All kinds of sinners in one room. Not to mention the bedrooms upstairs."

Now this last was an exaggeration. Annie had never run a house of ill repute, and there was rarely a fight between the tribes, white or red, but young city priests will believe anything.

"Well, do you think the hotel will continue now that Annie's gone?"

"Oh, I think there are a couple of people with their eye on that property too," I say, making it up.

The priest looks crestfallen.

I decide to press our advantage. "You have to admit it's a pretty building," I say. "All that brick."

"Yes, well...."

"Have you had any other offers?" Bob asks.

The priest looks weary in his shoulders, like the weight of this place might bring him to his knees at any moment. "No. None at all." He takes another sip; he doesn't bother raising his pinky finger this time.

"Course, the money may not matter, eh, father," I burst in again, "what with rebellion brewing in the town."

"Rebellion?"

"Oh yeah. Full scale twenty-first century Protest-antism," I say with deliberate emphasis on the first syllable. "Some are threatening to break away and set up a new denomination."

"Some folks are planning a hijack," Bob chimes in.

"A what?" The priest almost chokes on his lemon square.

Bob is staring at me in horror. How close should we get to the truth? I nod and wink.

"A takeover."

"A sit in."

"I hope you've decommissioned the place, unblessed it, whatever you call it," I say. "Don't delay getting shut of the place. Could get ugly."

"Deconsecrate." He clears his throat. "We have to deconsecrate it. Already scheduled, for Sunday."

"That's what I told Bob here. Nothing of the Holy Spirit remaining. Just superstition and sentimentality which you won't want to fall into the hands of former parishioners. They're libel to make a shrine of it."

Father Pat straightens suddenly, leans in. "Do those women who run the parish have anything to do with this?"

"I can't name names," says Bob. "They might seek reprisal, you understand." I give Bob another jab in the ribs. "Tempers are running hot. Violence is not out of the question!"

I have to jab him again. "But my information is that they are young people," he adds.

"But we hardly have any young people—"

"That's the rumour," I cut in and raise my eyebrows in the direction of the Mueller kid bobbing up and down in the back corner. The young Father follows where I lead before I continue: "Young people are an unpredictable element these days. They may want it for some kind of new age sect. Illicit purposes. Sex. Psychedelics, things like that."

Suddenly Bob finds surprising life in himself and goes for the jugular. "Understand, it's a liability," he parrots just like I've instructed. "I could take it off your hands. Avoid an embarrassing situation with the *media*." He whispers these last few words.

"The media! Okay, okay," says the priest, squeezing his big cross against his chest now. "What's your best offer?"

And Bob is ready this time without prompting. "Two thousand."

"Sold," barks the priest, his lemon square abandoned on his saucer, his tea still in its cup. "I'll talk to the bishop tomorrow. Let's shake on it." And so we do, right there by the teapots. And if the priest had turned around at that moment, he would have seen thumbs up around the room.

FLORENCE

Just as they shake hands on the deal, small cries go up everywhere around the room. Someone thumps Annie's table, and I swear I hear her speak. I don't know if the voice is inside me or outside me, but it's a pronouncement I hear, a prophecy, a gift, and I clutch myself to it like a mast to a ship: "Those who question will inherit the light."

DAISY

Before the night is done, after Father Pat has left, and everyone has had their fill of spirits and sandwich plates and squares, we get her into the coffin Bob fitted for her the very day of her death, without a pattern, just her measurements, all mitred and planed and varnished, not a board out of level. Jack supervises. It takes six of us. Two holding her feet, two holding her arms and two holding her head and shoulders to prevent any injury. Ever so carefully, like we are carrying a piece of China. Florence and I open the lid, holding it for balance. It weighs nothing. Simple birch, unlined, unadorned. Long thin boards. Air tight. Varnished clear and full of light. At the end, we throw her grandmother's crazy quilt on top and gently close the lid.

The pallbearers shoulder her the old-fashioned way from the hotel, out the back door, make a ragged procession to the sanctuary, cats from her home place in tow (some have taken up residence at the hotel since her death), all of us swaying and catching, traipsing over the lawn behind the hotel, zigzagging up the hill to the foot of the church, up the stairs, where Florence and I shoo the cats away, through the front doors and finally to the vestibule. Just like Annie herself has done for decades. Someone runs ahead to find the bier at the back of the church, an old wooden table they're using for the purpose, and moves it into the main aisle, just through the vestibule, into the church proper.

Funny, how back becomes front, how life becomes death, when turned around. How breaking bread and bearing becomes bier. How torn becomes mended or a pattern completely new.

Vera leads us in another round of hails and responses, this time to the psalm about dark valleys and pastures, mountaintops and feasts where cups of wine are taken. "Remember her," we murmur. And I can tell by the force of the words among us that we are praying just as much for ourselves as for Annie. So human to want to be remembered.

FLORENCE

Jack says he will stay the night again with the body. I offer to spell him off, but he says he must have one last night with her alone. Her spirit is still there. He can feel it he says. "I don't know what it is. I think she has something to say to me."

I nod my head. "The water," I say. Nodding at the baptismal font at the back of the church. "Try the water."

He laughs, his mind off somewhere, shakes his head. "Of course. The water. Thank you."

"Thank you, Jack Ramsey, for loving her." I take both his hands in mine and give them a squeeze. "I am truly sorry for your loss."

He does not reply right away but collects himself, looks down and looks up again. "Thank you."

I say, "Leave the casket open, I'll watch her."

The women are nervous about flies and birds and me.

I adopt my best farmer talk: "Go on with you," I say. "It's not my first time through."

I admit though it gets harder and harder: this giving and taking. This having to start all over again from scratch. From the smallest routines: when to get up in the morning, what bed to sleep in at night, how much to make for supper. To the largest: where to put these arms, this love I have for everything.

Florence closes the casket in the end. Closed or open, it is no matter to me. Her presence permeates this space. There is not a molecule of air without her mind directing it. I babble nonsense; I am an old man. Finally, they bow their heads, they bob, they duck, they leave me be.

After they're gone, I sit myself down in the last pew, just across from her. Stay long awake in the flickering of votives banked beneath the picture of the Black Virgin with the torn cheek. When their wicks start to sputter and give out, I lay myself down on the table beside her, my head toward the dying light. Wake suddenly. Find someone has draped me with a blanket. See the red electric light over the tabernacle; the light that never goes out. See that someone has lit fresh candles under the black-skinned Madonna while I've slept. Feel my face, wet with crying. Touch myself, tears, and then the wood at the base of the coffin beside my head. That is when I hear her.

I was wrong to make you hide our love.

Oh, Annie. I touch the wood again.

I didn't trust myself, Jack.

I heave inside. But there is worse, I want to say: *Beloved, what am I to do without you?*

I think I hear her laugh. *We constantly reinvent ourselves.*

I prop myself up on one side, my body pained by the effort, lean lightly into the wood. *Reinvent?*

Jack Ramsey, you know the story of the earth; you've always known it. And you know my story well enough.

Annie Gallagher, you are the most extraordinary woman.

Whoever we've loved, lives on in us. A piece of me, you. Always.

Annie, what do you mean?

You have to be the witcher now. You are.

And as soon as she's said the words, I feel the tug in my hands.

I want you to have my nana's old divining rod for practice.

And in my mind's eye, I see where it is hanging, in among the hooks for coats, just inside her back door.

For now, I need you to keep watch over me, Jack.

I wipe the tears from my face and touch the wood one last time. Something fierce and primal rises in me.

I move back my post to the opposite pew again, sit up straight. I nod off a few minutes, maybe an hour or two, wake again, this time to the voices of men, terse whispers, the rustle of robes behind me. Priests. The light of day streaming in the stained glass windows. I listen not to the words themselves but their pitch. Listen for a lament or dirge, the slightest whiff of pontificating. I'll not let them hurt her again. I wrap the blanket closer around me. I see the old man is kneeling on the floor by her side, his teeth chattering. I let him be in peace. That's when I notice the kid in the shadows, the pale arms limp, the face obscured. Kristian Mueller? The waif. Only there for the time it takes for the blink of an eye, and when I look again, gone.

II

FATHER PAT

When the bishop arrives Saturday morning, he wants to take one last tour of the church before the deconsecration tomorrow. I explain the funeral, hope it won't be a problem. "It's an odd situation. She never took communion or came for the Sacrament of Reconciliation, but she was there every Sunday. She was their water witcher," I say, lowering my voice and raising my eyebrows as we go inside.

The bishop dips his free hand into the baptismal font at the back of the church and crosses himself.

I know he doesn't want to draw attention to the church closing. No doubt there will be quite an audience at the funeral later today.

"Was she very old?" he asks in a hesitant voice.

"Yes, she was one of the oldtimers here."

"Well some of that generation..." he starts to say, then stops himself, as if he's pondering something.

"I know it's irregular, but it was that or a rebellion," I say.

He ignores me, says he wants to pray with the body. We start walking towards the nave.

"I've promised them a simple funeral, no bells or whistles, no eulogy, in keeping with the new Vatican protocol. No communion of course."

"Yes, yes." The old man waves my explanations aside. He's using a cane since I saw him last. The rumour is he has Parkinson's. He's old enough, in his eighties, and should be long retired. But everyone knows the Vatican requires a bishop's resignation at seventy-five but doesn't often accept it until they're on their deathbed.

"Let me pray with the body."

"Certainly." I take him by the sleeve and try to guide him to where the casket rests on an old table, just inside the main door to the body of the church. Halfway there he shakes me off.

"I can manage on my own."

I find an old prayer kneeler for him. That's when I notice Jack Ramsey is there too, sitting alone, in the corner of the church, praying. He has a blanket around his shoulders. He looks over at us and grimaces. I give him a quick nod and turn back to the bishop.

The chancellor told me to keep an eye on His Excellency. He didn't say why, just that he had concerns about him travelling right now. But the bishop insists that it's his duty to be with his people upon the closing of their church. He has only reluctantly accepted the recommendations of the consultants. The diocesan deficit has forced his hand.

Only when he struggles to open the top half of the casket, do I intervene. We have only just pried the lid upright when he gasps and takes a step back as if he's seen a ghost. He almost trips on the kneeler and with his good leg shoves it violently out of the way.

"God help me," he shudders.

I manage to catch the lid and set it down gently. I leave him leaning over the table like that and walk to the nearest pew and sit down. He stares and stares, shakes his head, finally turns to me, agitation in his voice, "Annie...? What was her family name?"

The bishop catches himself between his cane and the table and topples down on his knees to the bare floor.

I rush to him. "Bishop, are you all right?" But he waves me away before I can help him up. I am regretting my promise to the ladies and thinking I should have paid more attention to the chancellor's warning. All I need is for his Grace to drop dead on my watch.

"Leave me alone," he says, his voice wavering, one hand up to stop me, his face flush now. He knows her, he says. "Annie?"

"Gallagher," I reply.

"Leave me!" He almost shouts it this time. So I take my seat again in the last pew of the nave.

He hauls himself up on his cane, making the sign of the cross, staring, then praying frantically, whispering as if his life depends on it, alternating, watching silently, then praying. I see him jump back at one point, bring one hand to his face in surprise, study the sunlight streaming over the body, look down at the face. Kneel again. He kneels there for some time, waves me away each time I approach, till finally he brings himself up with both hands on the top of the cane, shouting through sobs, "Do not assist me. I am the most wretched of men!" Drags himself up the centre of the aisle and prostrates himself just short of the stairs surrounding the sanctuary and the altar, the red light of the tabernacle in his sights.

At the end I have to help him haul himself upright. I am beginning to understand the chancellor's concern.

The bishop says he has had some kind of spell. He just needs an aspirin. At the same time, he announces that he will preside at the funeral. I try to reason with him, "Bishop, you've had a busy week, and you have a big day ahead of you tomorrow with the closing of the church. Why not leave this one to me?"

"Nevertheless, I will preside at today's funeral."

"What is her name?" I call back to where I know he is hovering, thinking I'm going to totter over at any minute.

"Oh, but you know who I am."

I look. It is the woman. It is her voice.

"Annie Gallagher," Father Pat says quietly, coming up beside me, fixing me with a peculiar look, threatening to stay rooted there at my side if I don't say something.

"Thank you, Father, that will be all."

It is her all right. I lost track of her, the dusky skin, the high cheekbones, the sweetheart forehead, the full red lips, red even in death. But I've never forgotten the voice.

What's this? My hands are shaking. Here, better hide, inside my robes. Bow my head or the young priest will suspect my condition. Oh Mary, Mother of God, she was beautiful and so frightening to my young aspect. She was cause to fall, I convinced myself.

When she visited the confessional, her voice husky like her father's, her hands delicate like her mother's, so alive they danced when she spoke.

"Do you have bad thoughts?" I asked her once. It was a selfish question. The contrast of her blonde hair against her dark skin dazzled and dazed in the half darkness of the confessional. She had looked at me puzzled and thought hard before she answered.

"I get sad and pained inside when I think of my maman, Father. How bad a person I must have been that she left."

That's how I first learned that she had lost her mother. And I had looked away in embarrassment. What I had meant, what I had been thinking was that I had had bad thoughts about her.

Such a normal thing, sexual attraction. Forced celibacy, distorted by shame and years of denial can make us into small-minded, near-sighted creatures. Oh, how I agonized, felt terrible at my temptation, thought, *Oh! If I could just rid myself of the object of my desire.* "If your eye causes you to sin, pluck it out!" I couldn't sleep at night, couldn't get her out of my waking mind.

Here she is, her hair is combed straighter in death than I remember it in life, a lustrous white now.

Forgive me, Annie.

Father Leo. Her lips don't move.

My heart stops. Yes, I know the voice.

Do not be afraid.

It was me I wanted to lock up.

Yes.

And in her face I see my life flash back sixty-odd years. It's as if I've died for an instant and see myself as she would have seen me: young, confused, and foolish. Twenty-one years of age, newly ordained. My first parish.

You almost killed me, Father Leo. Again her lips don't move. But from somewhere comes a low cry, a near growl. *ArrRhh!* A sob.

It can't be. I force myself to make the sign of the cross on her forehead. Dead cold, nothing there. But at the flutter of an eyelash, I flinch. Calm now, patience my heart. I must remember the young priest. He's come up beside me once more, wondering if I've gone off the edge.

"I knew this woman," is all I say. "From when I was much younger. It's a shock. I just need a minute." He gawks. Impertinent youth. Finally, moves away again.

God forgive me, how I wanted her.

How you sent me away. God forgive me.

Father Leo, I see Lady Death in you.

How does she know? The brain cancer. Inoperable. I've written the Papal Nuncio.

But then I remember. The dead know everything.

I forgive you, Bishop Leo, but save your people.

Suddenly I'm gasping for air. I'm inside of somewhere with layers of brick and cement, long hallways, rows of beds, grey-striped feather pillows, rough cotton sheets, grey wool blankets, the windows high and small. And then I see the occupants of the place. Some have heads the size of overgrown cabbages, ears like cauliflowers and lips split. Some sit in bed with diapers, grown adults. Some are stunted and deformed and struggle to carry themselves along. Some are smiling and wanting to take my hand. They talk to the empty air. They talk nonsense.

They touch all the time, Father Leo. Annie is speaking to me now. *They touch. It's how they communicate. Afterwards, I saw what an education it was. Their gift.*

"Bishop, Bishop Leo! Wake up! Wake up! Are you all right?" Father Pat is shaking me, lifting me from the floor.

The church. My first church. I look up. They've lowered the ceiling — foam board now. All Douglas fir planking up there, long sixteen-foot boards. Can't buy wood like that anymore. Birch floors. An altar of cedar, all the way from the coast; a table, like they're meant to be, for a meal.

"In all my life, I haven't touched or been touched," I say aloud.

The young priest stares at me.

"TIAs," I say, struggling to recover my wits, to cover myself. "Small strokes, normal for someone my age. It's nothing. I haven't had one in weeks. Just the shock of so many years. Find me an aspirin, will you?" And that sends him off on a cause. By the time he gets back, I have it all planned out.

"I'll say mass today."

He gapes at me.

"There is one thing I'll need from you—" He's still sputtering by the time I dismiss him.

I follow the two black robes through the front door of the church Saturday morning. They don't even see me hanging out in the parking lot, the young one fussing around the old one. He keeps going on about something, looks like he has a rod up his ass. The old one keeps taking deep breaths and leaning on his cane coming up the stairs. I give them about two minutes lead time and then I slip inside. The young priest is sitting in the last pew looking straight ahead and the other is bent over the coffin that's on a small table, with his eyes closed, holding the big cross hanging from his neck for dear life. They both have a troubled kind of light over them, browns and greys, but it's changing near the coffin where the light is a different tone, calming, like at the wake. I head for the men's bathroom downstairs.

I didn't bother to walk home after the wake last night. Found some kid's lost rain jacket on the slides at the school, threw it over me, and slept in a corner of the sandbox. If Mom could see me now she'd say that I looked like death warmed over. And I would have joked, Well, I am going to a funeral.

I hope I look a mess; it's how I feel inside.

I woke up this morning knowing that I have to see this through. I have to go up to each and every one of her friends and her guy (that's going to kill me) and look them in the eye and tell them the truth and how sorry I am for what I've done. And at the end of it, I have to turn myself in to the police, plead guilty, the whole bit. It's what Mom would have wanted. And she would have told me to at least comb my hair.

The first person I have to confess to though is Miss Annie. I have to sit with her for a while, and even if she can't hear me, apologize. I have to get up close to her and tell her everything.

About the magpies and the drugs, about Kelsey. God, I'm going to start crying again. I flush the toilet, splash cold water onto my face, and tuck my shirt into my jeans. Take the comb out of my back pocket.

I wait till I hear the Old Robe's cane ra-ta-tating on the floor overhead, the big front doors open and close again and the two of them stumping their way back down the stairs. Then I steal upstairs, slowly passing through the doors into the main part of the church, where Miss Annie's body is. That's when I see her guy, in the other back pew, on the other side, wrapped up in an old blanket, snoozing softly. I try to get as close to the coffin as I can, but I know I'll explode if I get too close. So I keep to the shadows and stand at attention, whispering everything I can.

ANNIE

It was a strange place, the institution, the children like moths coming to light. They would cling to you or shun you. They knew every feeling that passed your face, every shadow of intention, affection, whim. From our keepers I learned the categories of a subhuman being. Imbecile, Idiot, Moron. From the kept, I learned other forms of intelligence.

Hints of malice, meanness made them angry. Injustice was their bread. You were an open book. They knew at a touch what your intentions were. They saw your true heart. No one could hide from them.

"Annie's mad," said one of them the night I arrived. It was the best of words. I was enraged, but out of my mind too. That first night I lay on my black iron bed, covered with the same blue-striped spread as everyone else's, facing the wall with my back towards them, my knees up to my chin.

"Someone's hurt her very bad," said another and hugged me, not with a hug like we know it, but until her arms were too tired. I counted the minutes on the clock. Extraordinary was the comfort they gave to each other.

From them I learned which staff to avoid, which to trust. Some of the assistants treated them as their own children, but some waited and watched for who they could steal away. The ones who couldn't talk. The ones who couldn't move. There were soul stealers in that place. The children knew — you could see it in their sad eyes.

I used to help feed and dress the smaller ones. Their mouths didn't work right, swallowing was hard for them. They had things wrong with their hands or they hadn't been taught yet how to use them. Most were the tribe of the rejected with neither intelligence nor strength to understand the why of it. They lived with an unknown wound whereas I knew my labels. Delinquent. Bad influence. Wayward. Mental Defective.

They would look at me, longing on their wide flat faces. "Annie wanna play?" There were days I wished I could be like them.

That first night at the training school, the warden set me down on a stool, put an empty porridge bowl on my head and cut my long, pale, unruly hair. Pixie cuts were easier to control for head lice, and why I dreamed in that place of what I couldn't have.

That's when I learned the training school had been a finishing school at the turn of the century. An old staff telling a new staff the history. Girls from hundreds of miles around, girls from the flat prairie, set down in a small town, brick and mortar six stories high, by a river that fed a pot and kettle landscape, small streams and lakes rimmed with bluffs of poplar and spruce, traversed by muddy roads in spring. After World War I, the Presbyterians had sold it to the army to use as a hospital for shell-shocked veterans.

After I was shorn, they issued me a plain cotton brassiere, dressed me in a long white blouse with short puffy sleeves and a grey skirt that stopped just above the knees. Then they gave me a pair of white bloomers that stuck out below the hem and had to be fastened at the waist with a clothespin because they were too big for me. A safety pin was considered a dangerous weapon in the hands of a defective. Over top of these layers the girls were forced to wear a blue gingham jumper with cap sleeves that acted like an apron.

By day we did cross-stitch, and cooked and cleaned, and had choir. On special occasions us girls went down to the nearby Catholic convent for tea: New Year's Day, Mother's Day, Thanksgiving. The nuns always wanted to know who the Catholics were among us; I kept my mouth shut.

There were others like me, knowing their labels, rid of by a judge claiming to protect the morality of a community, a parent wanting a new marriage, or by a family who had fallen on hard times and couldn't support them, which was much in the thirties. Each of us coped in our own ways. Some were obedient nurse's pets, friends of everyone. Sometimes, in our beds at the end the day, a few of us spoke in whispers about where we were from, what we had left behind. But most of the time, I kept to myself and preferred my own imaginings.

I could see ghosts; though at first I didn't know that they couldn't be seen, that they were dead invisible to others. I had to be careful not to answer their greetings out loud. Some of the residents knew and some of the cleaning staff. There was a solidity to the ghosts like they were real people, but dressed wrong for the time and place. Day or night, it didn't seem to matter, they spoke to me.

One was a young woman, the daughter of a judge, who had been sent there to break her secret engagement to a country farmer. After a year he had married another. She had picked small field stones, collected them in her apron, one by one, and stitched them into the wide hem of her very best dress, a dark red, with heavy thread. One morning early she had donned the dress, walked into the river and set herself down. Some said her ghost slept nights in what served then as our parlour and served in her life as the sewing room. That her dark visage still walked between the fields and the river at the crack of dawn.

"How did you know that?" One older cleaning woman had grabbed my hand and looked around for anyone within earshot when I had first approached her, frightened out of my wits. When I didn't answer her, she tried to make light of it. "It was a long time ago, when ladies were foolish creatures and men were foolisher."

You soon learned you couldn't tell the nurses. They moved you to the psychiatric ward, shot you through with tranquilizers. "You've got second sight," an old cook told me finally, "but don't tell no one here. It'll only bring you trouble."

After the ladies, came the broken young men, truckloads of them wandering around dozing on their feet. My father had told me about the ghosts of the dead on the battlefield, so I knew who they were when we first met. How they rose to charge the Germans from the same trenches where they'd fallen a week or a year before. How they warned those still living, of the enemy in this trench or the mines hidden in the field. How they succoured the wounded, carrying them to clearing stations, talking all the time to keep them conscious, fed them from rations and canteens full of fresh water.

My father used to tell the old priests who came to the bar, the scriptures are wrong where they said that the dead no longer look like themselves. Yes, they are no longer a body, but they look like themselves, the image of themselves, down to the same rings on their fingers, the scapulars on their neck, the cigarette case in their hand, the St. George's medal hanging from their throat. Even their tag numbers. The timbre of their voices. The same. They were instantly recognizable.

One soldier was said to have hung himself in the pantry at the training school. The old cook swore meat would spoil if you let it thaw on those shelves. Several convalescents had never left the institution. They'd left their very souls in the walls, the staff said.

I heard them some nights. Young men groaning, frightened by sudden movements, loud sounds. Hungry for earth times. "Larks," they told me. Larks were singing and shells exploding as men were screaming, falling among the orchards, with green apples. The dying screams of men, the mating songs of birds joined. Friends drawn and quartered by a shell.

And so we suffered the dying young men, their dreams fused with ours. "Haunting us who still have our wits and those who haven't," the old cook said. Even animals, dumb beasts, can sense the texture of grief. I made what offerings I could: a handful of strawberries, a robin's feather, a prayer.

Nights in my bed when all was quiet, I pretended I was Rapunzel. I lay waiting for my hair to grow long enough and one of the young soldiers to come by my window. We'd make rope of my long hair and tie it off on the bed post and he would take me away from this place, take me home to my father. But by morning waking, my hair was cut short again.

12

FLORENCE

The bishop barely makes it through the front door of the hotel when he throws himself to the floor, beating his breast as he falls and landing hard on his knees. Vera, Daisy, and me are sitting at the Table of Truth, moved back out to its original home by the postal wicket, already drinking our Saturday morning coffee. We think the man's had a stroke and all get up at the same time, to help His Grace off the hardwood. He begins to address us.

"I am the most wretched of men! I am not worthy to touch the hem of your cloaks."

Vera makes it to him first, crouches down. "Your Grace!"

"No, leave me here. This is where I must be, for I have come to wash the feet of the women disciples. I have so much to repent."

"But Bishop," Daisy tries to intervene.

"No. I speak the truth. I am out of my mind with grief, but I know fully the sin I have committed.

"Please bring me a basin of water, towels, and a washcloth. I am sorry I cannot carry it myself, that I must rely on you for that." The poor man is breathing heavily.

Vera gets up and does as he says.

Then he asks us to push our chairs together and make a small circle in one corner, off to the side. We take off our shoes and our socks, such as they are. Daisy has only her sandals.

We are all of us, the bishop included, already sobbing before he even lifts a cloth. Such is the feeling among us. A kind of joy, I try to explain to the men afterwards, wondrous, like everything that day. The water of tears and the water of our washing mingling. "Isn't that what you call an absolution in your religion?" Buster teases me. "Only usually it's done on women by priests, not the other way around and without the washing," the grand order of things, the irony not lost on him.

One by one the bishop washes our feet. Each dip of water, each stroke of the cloth, he tells us something of the story of his tortured actions with regards to Annie Gallagher. We tell him the parts of the story we know, our own and Annie's mingled together, and of how she ended up, a water witcher. His tears, more liquid than the water by the end of it. "Purified," I said later. We and him washed in salt.

Finally, Vera is the one to appeal to his common sense. "Bishop, we need you to be able to stand through a full funeral today, an hour, maybe more. Let me help you off that floor."

Oh yes, yes." He seizes the chair she brings him, then grasps the coffee I hand him and drinks greedily. Daisy removes the wash water not to the sink but out the back door, where she pours it over a flowerbed.

The first time my father saw my mother, he told me, the vines that curled around the doorposts where she stood were dark with fruit. The walnut trees were full. The apples, the pears, the yellow plums were ready to be picked. The walled gardens, shot through here and there from mortars, were planted with lettuce and radish and cabbage, hollyhocks and roses growing taller and fuller than any he'd seen back home.

My father said she was from a place of old cities that remembered waves of occupation in their very foundations: Celtic, Roman, Frank, and Viking; pagan and Christian. A place where civilization had prospered for thousands of years before Majestic had even been settled. A place of art and eight-hundred-year-old churches, all of them made from stone, hewn in the traditional way. A place for opera and theatre. Grand gardens with plants collected from the four corners of the world and laid out in the manicured French fashion.

Before the war, Lorraine was a place where almost anything grew without effort. Afterwards, all that was left were craters as treacherous as quicksand, oozing with rains, coughing up bits of barbed wire, unexploded shells, and putrid bodies. A colossal ossuary, a bone field that snaked for miles.

My father told me that she was not much older than seventeen when they met at Bar Le Duc on the approach to Verdun, the road they called La Voie Sacree, *the Sacred Way,* because it was the only way by some miracle still open to the front and the lone reason the Canadians were holding the line. She stood on the threshold of an *estaminet,* wearing the black of mourning, common to the women of that time, no hat, her long hair tucked up at the nape of her neck, a basket in hand. She was smiling. The allied reinforcements had arrived and they were packing in supplies day and night.

When there was a halt called in the line, my father said, their eyes caught and held. My mother reached out to stroke the face of his horse. She looked so thin, my father offered her some of his rations. There were tears in her eyes as she accepted and gave a little bow.

They met again by chance, he said, in Paris. From then on, all my father wanted was to protect her and there was no question that she would come home with him. After that he took all his leaves in Paris.

FLORENCE

When Father Pat arrives early to vest for the funeral, I feel compelled to prophesy. I swear to the others later, I felt moved. I'm not sure what moves me. Maybe it's the events of these last days, the BSE plague of these last weeks, maybe the drought of these past three years, coming now to a critical point in Annie's passing. Maybe it's me playing my devilish part to help Daisy and Buster and Mike to keep the priest occupied and out of the way for the Project. Maybe it's the humility of the older priest I've just witnessed that has made me bold. Or my schoolteacherly orneriness. Maybe it is the Holy Spirit and the Holy Spirit is all of these things.

It's Daisy Goodchild's job to lay out his vestments, change the altar cloth, find the readings in the lectionary, and set up the microphone. I'm just here to help her with a bit of folding and sorting.

"Such a wind there is today, Father, blowing the living green branches off everything. As if there's a hundred thousand souls out there wanting in."

"Yes, Florence, yes," he says absentmindedly, glancing at me over his glasses, standing with one leg bent, flipping through the sacramentary to find his prayers. Like in the old days, like turning the clock back in time, like when I was a small child, these priests, their noses in books all the time, praying words on a page, forgetting to pray the people.

"The Son of Man has nowhere to lay his head, I tell you." I raise my voice and I don't stop raising it. "Not the creatures of the world, not even the foxes or the birds: the ducks, the swans, the geese. This year's migration none of them stayed, they didn't even stop. I saw them – clouds of them – all spring, circling overhead, riding the thermals, trying to spot a patch of water. Pretty soon, they pulled up their tails, headed north. All except for the magpies that is. The magpies will stay through summer and winter; they never leave."

They never mass, I almost add. I'm not sure how they've survived the drought; maybe they fly to water? It doesn't matter. I have his attention now and Daisy's too. The young priest looks up from his book of prayers. Daisy has stopped mid-stride, prayer stole on her arm, her eyes playful around the edges, her mouth round, threatening to giggle.

"The weather in these times, Father, is epic." I don't know why I'm forced to speak. But I want him to hear this testament. To take it forward with him when he leaves this place.

"We're witnessing a fundamental change. Lightning storms at the crack of dawn. What killed our Annie." I cross myself. "Windstorms, Father, in the middle of a clear summer's day, the sky as blue as blue can be. Winds that blow nothing but dirt and air and bear no moisture, not a cloud. Only one other time in living memory when that happened in these parts." I know I have taken on the voice of the dead.

He's shook up now. He's distracted, but good.

"The Great Depression, Father. The dust bowl. Like when Annie and I were growing up. Only we've got it summer and winter. A sign of biblical proportions. It's not a good sign, Father. It's not a good sign at all."

Ever since I got here, that's all I hear about. The winters not as cold, not as much snow. The falls wetter, the springs and summers hotter and drier. The extremes of moisture. Everything's backwards. They keep telling me, looking to me, but I don't have any magic for them. I can't dig them any wells like their friend, Annie. It's one of the reasons I'm glad to leave this place. I don't know how to help. All I have to offer is doubt, doubt about myself more than anything, and a fistful of rules. I doubt myself, which is more dangerous than any other lack of faith.

BUSTER

I knock twice, twice again, then wait. Goofy signals — the women-folk's idea with the plan moved up by one day with Annie's funeral. I nearly drop my pants when the young Father opens the back door of the church. My eyes bug out of my head, like a badger caught stealing into someone else's burrow. Instinctively, I want to duck and hide. Instead I grunt, try to look nonchalant. I've always wanted to see what was behind the altar. Not much to it from this angle. Shelves, a closet, a few cupboards, a couple of sinks, one with a big sign over it: "Mass wine and holy water here." A curtain in the corner. One looks like an exit stage front. I want to look closer in the cupboards, but Father Pat is assessing my curiosity.

"Buster is here to give us a hand with some of these vestments," Daisy calls over her shoulder, nonchalant-like too. We had told him we were getting the linens cleaned and mended before handing them over to the Diocese. Florence smiles and gives me a little wave, the closest thing to a wink from that woman.

"Yes, indeedy," I say. "Let's see how much you've got to carry, my girl, then we can join the — group," I almost stumble. I was thinking "the party," but that wouldn't be proper under the circumstances.

Mrs. Cummins is trying to play the organ again. That's what I tell Daisy every time I hear her. I've attended enough weddings and funerals and midnight Masses here to know. She doesn't play, she tries to play. This time, though, there's a purpose to the cacophony. They know it will keep him away from the sanctuary till the last possible minute.

"Now Father, you were going to check on the bishop before you vest, weren't you? And don't forget the pallbearers. Still an hour till the service." Daisy steers him past me. He swallows it like a lamb.

"See you in a bit, Father." I make sure to pump his hand on the way by.

When he's gone, Daisy whispers, "Mike's already started." I just nod and slip through the curtains. Not much reason to come inside a Catholic Church over the years. The odd wedding or funeral, like today. Daisy's the Papist in the family. I'm just a token member of the United Church.

The young Mueller fellow is there too, near the back, though I'm not too worried about any confrontation from that quarter. He looks pretty absorbed in himself, still twisted up like a cork, rubbing his hands together, and tapping his foot like there's no tomorrow. I give him a military salute, as if to say I'm glad you're keeping the faith. He cracks his knuckles, gives me a quick nod, goes back to staring at the floor, rocking himself back and forth.

No sign of Jack. Mike says he went home to catch some rest.

Mike's on a ladder, unscrewing the Stations of the Cross. "Here," he says, motions me towards all the cardboard on the floor, the roll of unbleached paper, the utility knife and the tape gun.

"Help me wrap this up."

We work through all the stations that way. Jesus: falling and falling and falling, Veronica wiping his face, the soldiers nailing him to the cross. It's a good story this way, handing it down, laying a cover of protection over it.

We take turns on the ladder, passing each scene down, wrapping it, till we get to the big picture of the Madonna with the scar under her eye. An awful lot of pain in this religion, that's what I've always said to Daisy. Every Tom, Dick, and Harry grimacing or dead. She always says back, "There's an awful lot of pain in this life." And there's nothing I can say to that. Except that I've always liked the look of that Madonna, dark and alive, her eyes piercing right through you. We fold her up like all the rest, blank newsprint up against the paint, wrapped in thin cardboard and sealed with packing tape. Load them all in the box I have under my arm. Convey them past the lone communion rail, the altar, to the priest's quarters again. Daisy stops us at the back door to give the all clear and we move them into the back of Mike's camper. Later, after the funeral is over and everyone is gone, we plan to take them down the hill to the hotel for storage in the back pool room.

MIKE

I do recall the first holy pictures I saw. The nuns would give out small cards with a Mary or a Joseph or a Jesus on them. Oftener than not Jesus had blond or brown hair and blue eyes and creamy-coloured skin, wore white billowing robes and looked happy. Joseph always looked the more sombre of the two, like someone who had found himself in a tight spot but had shouldered his responsibilities. Mary was always serene, like nothing rattled her. If you did well at catechism, if you answered a question right in class, if you scored high on the test, if you made your first communion, you would get a picture card. Each one had a story and a little prayer on the back.

There was Bernadette and the devotees of the Lady of Lourdes. Dark swarthy complexions, black eyes and olive skins, the way all mountain girls must look I imagined. Any of them could have been my best friend on the playground; each one, brave and pious.

Lourdes herself had roses growing at her feet and rays of light escaping from her crown of gold as if she were the sun itself. The heavens in her picture were like a prairie heaven, big black thunderclouds arrayed behind her. Little sheep drinking from her waters.

Fatima had skin and robes whiter than light, had rosaries wrapped around her praying hands, had little shepherd children kneeling at her feet, swaddled in rough clothes.

Saint Terese de Lisieux, the Little Flower, had a crown of flowers surrounding her pale, sharp, and sweet face, full of good jokes. They said she was always teasing her sisters.

All of them, mistresses of the sun.

We never had money for pictures in the glass windows in Majestic. Just a tint or two of pastel in the top panes at St. Joseph's. The stations every Lent. It was encouraged every Friday, some Sundays, after mass to do the stations, contemplate them and pray the rosary. The ladies in the CWL would lead.

It's been a long time since I was an altar boy, years since I was behind the altar even to make an announcement. I think all this as Buster and I lift and carry the images back and forth between us, until the walls are bare and all of the faces are gone. Swiftly and silently until we've helped Daisy remove the chalices and vestments, all except the ones we usually use. It's as if we're powered by unseen hands, familiar hands, I want to say to Buster, hands we've known but can't place, until, on the last go, I dip my hand in the baptismal font to bless myself.

At the institution the boys worked in the fields, but they wouldn't let the girls go outside. Only on special outings: a wiener roast, a picnic, a sports day, trips between the school, the gymnasium for physical education, an errand to fetch vegetables from the garden. When they did let us out, I made myself a bed of grass along the edge of the playground and lay on the earth and listened to the faint rumblings of flowing water. That was how I came to know I was different. I couldn't be cut off from water for long.

I stood in the shower long after others had finished, stood with my head under the tap, letting the water cradle me, my eyes closed, thinking of streams and rivers, of aquifers, and the pipes snaking through that old building. But the sheerest force of water in that place wasn't to be found in the pipes. The sheerest force of water was to be found in human form.

A ward full of water, swollen heads on pillows, twelve lined up against both walls, ventilators plugged into their throats and tubes running in and out of their noses and arms. Their open mouths like red flowers, their eyes, wells.

Water on the brain, the housekeeping staff called it. Vegetables. Never moving, their stares fixed straight ahead, their bodies growing under them, still defecating. Their heads were wondrous. Oceans in those heads. How many rivers?

It was easy to slip by the night aides, the wheel of keys on their waists. I hid in the shadows. The doors could be jigged to not quite close. Big doors, heavy, slow to swing. I was a skinny, slippery sliver of nothing in those days. I slipped through a crack, pulled back covers, slid down, and laid my ear by one of those heads, by the rushing of the waves. Sea sleep. The best sleeps I had in that place. Mornings they found me, bed clothes tangled with tubing.

It did not last long.

Deranged, delusional, they wrote.

Admonished. You shouldn't. You mustn't. Till I would go there walking in my sleep. Then they started to restrain me at night, wrist straps, foot straps, bedding short shrift. The more they held me, the more I wanted to run.

But the water never left me. I had oceans in my belly, lakes and the river so close. I could feel it rising in me whenever I got to open ground, through my feet, my open hands, it was the most natural feeling. No one wondered why except that they thought I was an imbecile. Wandering with my hands outstretched, following the rivers inside of me. The only concession, that they left me to wander barefoot in the grass in summer because we had to save our shoes for winter.

For a long time I didn't understand it, these feelings I would have under the strangest circumstances. When it rained, when I was near a river, like the sound of an old lullaby that I knew once and was trying to remember.

"You're a diviner," an old German woman attendant told me when she saw me head down, pacing the grass or when she found me sitting by the river. "Don't tell no one here. They'll think you're crazy. Lock you up forever."

And so I kept the ocean inside of me.

VERA

The pallbearers keep Father Pat busy at the hall until the last possible minute with all kinds of questions about the service and the procession afterwards. I can imagine the conversation, them playing the part of dumb country hicks, him taking up the role of Chief Enlightener. I am in the vestry waiting for him when he returns. He looks at his watch, glances at me, hurries to the table where his ceremonial robes are laid out and throws them on.

I hand him the jar just as he pulls on his prayer stole. "It's water, Father, just a little thimbleful from some of the wells she's dug over the years." Those waters we could gather in time, mingled now from all those places, I think. But I don't say this.

He stops fussing with his stole. "It's not holy water."

"But Father, think about it. In this time of drought, every drop is holy. It's a way for the people to give thanks."

"No, it's a way for some to draw attention to this confounded woman's gifts and deprive Him who is the rightful heir of any glory His due."

"Who created water if not God, Father? And isn't God the source of such gifts?"

"But it hasn't been blessed by the church."

"You could sanction it, Father." With the touch of your hand and the sign of the cross over it, I was going to say, or the tap of your wand. But I bite my tongue, take a deep breath, "With your blessing."

He sighs. "Oh, very well, just this one time. But there is a danger, Vera, of the people equating the gift with the life, of forgetting who is the true font of eternal life and all gifts, the Lord Jesus Christ. The sacraments are not some kind of superstitious mumbo jumbo."

"But we are the only hands God has, Father. Isn't that true?"

He grudgingly grants me that.

"Vera, I know we have not always seen eye to eye. But let this be a gesture of my goodwill to you and the congregation, that I want to leave on good terms."

"And so do we all, Father — want to end well," I say quickly.

He fixes me with a funny look then but recovers himself.

"You'll use it today then? During the rites?"

"I'll use it."

"Thank you."

"But I won't be drawing any special attention to it. It's not the miracle of the witching we're celebrating today. It's the miracle of the resurrection."

"Yes, Father," I understand.

With that I pour the collected waters into the vessel he uses for the purpose, a large ice bucket, but pure brass, and hand it to him, with a fresh willow switch for the sprinkling.

"Maybe today we should use the brass sprinkler," he starts.

I stop for a minute. "That would mark a departure for you, Father. You always ask for a branch when it's in season."

"Well, yes, you're right. Never mind."

I had sent Daisy and Kelsey to collect the roses from the hotel.

"I've got to see to the flowers out front," I say brightly, picking up the bucket and branch, wanting to exit before he can change his mind. "People are starting to arrive."

ANNIE

I was the cook's helper in the kitchen, chopping pots of carrots and parsnips and potatoes. She put me in charge of the other girls, plucking chickens and gutting fish. I was a dab hand, she said. It was hard times, Depression years, hard to get anything; even salt and pepper were scarce. We had to grow what we needed: cows for fresh milk and cream, chickens for roasting, beets and turnips for the cellars, pails of peas, green beans, and wild raspberries canned, put up on shelves. Apples stored in the root cellars. I was good at it, and I might have stayed forever but for the trip to Ponoka.

All the month after my insides ached, my cramps were heavier, blood everywhere. Spotting, the aides called it. "You're spotting," as if it were a refinement. It was later, when I heard them talking amongst themselves, that I found out I could never get pregnant.

That's when I ran away to the city. At first the kitchens of old hotels, then their backrooms washing dishes, prostituting myself when rent money was short, playing pickpocket, doing whatever I had to. That's when the drinking started. Four years till I was of legal age, and I could go home of my own accord.

It was only when I came back to these parts that I began to remember myself. And people who'd known my grandmother came by asking. I thought on all my nana had taught me – the dawn, the green willow, the marking of the streams, the pull. I practiced on nights when the moon was full and the currents rose strong in the ground, with my hands remembering, my nana's spirit guiding me. I began to witch.

13

MIKE

The people sit straight against the pews in their Sunday clothes and polished heels waiting for the Saturday afternoon service to begin. Others, with dirt under their nails and callouses on their hands, are shaking their heads, digging at the hard floor with their steel toe and rubber-soled boots. The men play with the brims of their hats, the women rearrange their skirts, impatient for this part of the burying to be over. Jack has joined the choir in the loft, one of the few tenors among them every Sunday. I don't know how he puts up with Mrs. Cummins' playing. Says he likes to sing and has an obligation to sing, especially today, to give Annie the best send-off.

Some notice the stations gone, the saints' pictures, and exchange indignant words back and forth. "The nerve of the bishop. They've already started the decommissioning!" But they keep their voices low and pleasant; it is Annie Gallagher's funeral after all. Others feel the difference too, but they put it down to the roses, the pots of them on the windowsills and in the sanctuary. How they alter the appearance of this place.

Before they bring the casket up from the back of the church, people stand out of respect. The pallbearers, Vera and the two Fathers form a circle around the coffin, where it sits on a small table, waiting. Vera welcomes the people and pronounces the greeting: a word of hope, a word of faith, a word of community as the rubrics proscribe and yet not as proscribed. Father Pat has agreed to this since Vera is the chair of the parish council, and as a concession, since he insisted on choosing all the readings and the music for Annie's service today. Normally her family would do that, but since she has no family...

At the foot of the church, at the join where the aisles meet east and west, north and south, Vera raises her voice above the crowd, turns as she speaks so that everyone front and back, inside and outside can hear:

"Friends and neighbours, Annie Gallagher has passed from us. What shall we say of her? A woman of suffering, a woman of strength." A murmur goes through the crowd as people pass the message down the stairs out the back of the little church, from lips to lips, to where people are lined up into the parking lot. "What shall we remember? A woman of considerable gifts. A woman with generous hands. How shall we go on? Together as she would have liked it, celebrating her life on earth and her life to be."

Vera always speaks so well. The young priest pulls a face, keeps trying to catch her eye. The old bishop starts to clap, awkwardly, against his hip, one hand still on his cane, bowing to her slightly, grinning and making strange utterings, something about her being a deaconess in the making. She gives him a big smile.

Everyone else says "Amen."

Then the bishop picks up the willow branch from the bucket Kelsey has held out to him, flings water at the casket, throws it vigorously, almost drunken-like, swaying on one lame leg. Father Pat, the younger of the two, looks bewildered, tries to check the old man's enthusiasm and take the branch from him. The old bishop dodges his reach, keeps walking in circles around the casket, three, five, seven, an irregular number of times, sprinkling the holy water on Annie until all of us are powerfully silent.

We strain towards the action, start to breathe faster. I catch Vera's eye, Daisy's, Alex's. Alex is sitting in the aisle seat, back pew, his usual spot, Mike is right across from him. Best friends and ushers for life; that's the joke. Daisy and I are close to the front, owing to the reading we have to do. I can tell some want to jump out of their pews, out of their places, want to hold her last witching branch in their hands and join the old bishop in dancing the water. Bob found the wand by her side, somehow knew how important it was when he brought it to me, said even him an unbeliever, who did not worship things or in a church, could see that it must be preserved.

I had passed it on to Vera who put it in a vase of water to keep till morning, and then passed it on to the young Father who isn't any the wiser.

ANNIE

I hear the waters calling *Come home. Stay with us.* The call I've heard since a child. *Abide by this earth.* The waters in all their voices, their individual strands rising up in a single singing, at once a harmony and a dissonance of whistles and flutes below the earth, the gathering of streams, a chorusing of angels, yes, a chorusing in all the realms.

At the back door, Kelsey unfolds the pall, the white cloth. And with his one free hand and the altar girl's help, the old bishop lays it over the casket, fumbles over his shepherd's crook to rearrange it carefully, gently, where the droplets of water have soaked through. Then the young priest signals to Mrs. Cummins and the choir up in the loft, where Jack is too, and the pallbearers. Hurry up, the young Father seems to say with his eyes, let's get on with it, and Mrs. Cummins is sailing us up the aisle. People who haven't sung in years open their mouths, know the words.

Holy God we praise thy name.
Lord of all we bow before thee.

At "Infinite" all the sweetness of voices pooling from the low note to high, the contrast of men's and women's voices straining to come together and coursing on.

Infinite thy vast domain.
Everlasting is thy reign.

Then in repetition:

Infinite thy vast domain,
Everlasting is thy reign.

A verse and another chorus and we are up the aisle, in spirit if not in body, with Annie, all of us at the foot of that altar, waiting for our commendation. It was as if all our waters were going out to her, carrying her along the one great human river home to the mouth, towards which we all strain and long.

They place her coffin a few steps from the six-foot Paschal candle and finish the ceremonial preparations. Kelsey brings the book of the gospels, then the cross. All of it they lay on top of the white pall on top of her box.

After the procession, Father Pat starts pacing up and down the aisle, wringing his hands, looking to the back door, motioning for people to come forward, astounded with all the mourners who have come, standing in the back on each side, milling in the foyer, spilling out on to the front steps.

"Make room, make room," he urges as firmly as his sense of decorum will allow. "Please slide down. Let's seat as many as possible."

Why is he surprised? It's the whole country she's dug wells for, found water for, fed herbs to. The people have come to the Mount to pay their last respects. She's a legend. For a priest, he's surprisingly unpastoral.

It takes the bishop to bring some levity to the situation:

"A few loaves of bread and a few fishes," he calls out from the altar steps, "and we can feed everyone."

People start to move in closer, cozy up with their neighbour. People in the choir loft and in the lobby, squeeze shoulder to shoulder, push forward, line the aisles on both sides of the church. Alex and Mike stand at each side of the main door, looking back over the crowd and waving people forward.

"That's right," the bishop pronounces. "Come in out of the wind," for even then it was threatening to blow. "And close the door behind you."

Kelsey opens the big red book and stands with it in front of the bishop. He bows his head and speaks without glancing at the page.

"My dear people, let us pray. Oh Heavenly Father, we believe that even though we die, we will rise on the last day. Grant that through the mystery of Annie Gallagher, our sister...." He stops and looks around himself as if he's surprised by what he's about to say.

"Our dear sister Annie, who has gone to her rest in Christ, will rise with him on the last day."

Father Pat starts to say, "Amen," to hurry him along, but the bishop raises his hand and closes his eyes again.

"We look to your glory, oh Heavenly Father, through your Son, Jesus the Christ, our Lord, who lives and reigns with you and the Holy Spirit, Three in One, the Blessed Trinity, forever and ever, Amen."

Then it dawns on me: the altar table, the procession of gift-bearers, the coffin just at the foot, Annie presiding over us all. Annie was and still is the Table of Truth in this place.

14

DAISY

It's Florence's job to read the epistle, but the old bishop walks up to the podium, flips the book open, studies the page marked by the green ribbon, turns to the next leaf, studies some more till finally at the bottom he finds what he's looking for. He lifts it slightly out of its place so that you can just see its green velvet cover. The one I embroidered the edges of with gold thread and Celtic knots. The Book of Infinity I call it.

Florence stands to one side, at the bottom of the steps, waiting for him to call her, but he doesn't. Father Pat clears his throat, tries to catch his eye, but the old man can't be caught. It's peculiar what takes place next and people would later say it was all part of God's plan and the first sign that a miracle was about to occur.

The old bishop removes his hat, sets it on a shelf under the podium, and starts to read from the Song of Songs. *Arise my beloved, my beautiful one and come!* There's glee in his eyes. He lets his staff clatter to the floor.

For see, the winter is past,

Someone in the back titters. It is sweet to watch him, an old man excited about young love. It's a reading you hear at a wedding not a funeral. For heaven sakes, we did read this at our wedding! I look for Buster in the crowd. He's smiling too. Father Pat starts to crease his cassock with his hands, to bore a hole in the floor with his glare, trying to be patient, trying to keep the red heat from rising to his face, but too late.

The flowers appear on the earth,

Father Pat had chosen a considerably unremarkable reading about God taking care of his flock, his weak sheep, and so on and so forth.

and the song of the dove is heard in our land.

We do have doves here, mourning doves we call them. Known by their sad coo coo coos, their feathers, a delicate, pearly grey. I love the sound of them out the window on a summer's morning, early, just as we're making love.

FLORENCE

When I get up here I realize the bishop is determined to read so I just stay to the side and wait it out. I know he'll eventually see me and come to his senses.

When we met this morning, he was shaking like a white poplar in spring. It was such a shock when he insisted on washing our feet. He told us how many feelings he had coming back to this place, how there were so many memories for him here, how it had hit him between the eyes that he had known Annie. How much he had wondered about her over the years. He says he remembers me too, that I used to go to confession every chance I got. I was always sorry for something in those days, sorrier than most children my age, heavy in my regret, but he never knew why.

I took him under my wing. I told him, "Not to worry, Bishop. We're all a little emotional today. It's been a shock. We appreciate your coming to share our sorrow." He was speechless at that and just patted my hand as best he could while leaning on his cane, kneeling the way he was on the floor.

BUSTER

When he starts to read there's a chuckling at the back. Alex will say it's the Protestants. I admit the words sound odd coming out of the mouth of a celibate clergyman. The bishop looks delighted with himself, all that flowery lover talk. I know, the lover is Jesus and the beloved is the soul, and so on and so forth – Daisy's trained me up good. But still.

O my dove in the clefts of the rock,
in the secret recesses of the cliff,

"Hmm. Hmm. Hrumph." The old bishop stops himself mid-sentence.

Hah, even he thinks it's queer.

Let me see you,
let me hear your voice…"

When he gets to the end, he sees Florence waiting to read and Daisy behind her. He gets flustered and realizes he's in the way and that he's made a mistake. But he seems seized by something and can't help himself. He calls up Daisy. Florence keeps squeezing her hands together in front of her, as if she's afraid they might fly apart if she lets them be, but she smiles and steps aside.

The old bishop shows Daisy something in the book, where he's moved the red ribbon – points at the place on the page, looks her in the eye and waits till she nods. He smiles and pats her on the back then totters off the risers, almost hopping like a jack rabbit to take a seat in the front row. People make room. He lays his cane on the floor in front of him. Father Pat looks fit to be tied watching from his perch on the altar, his arms folded across his chest. He tries to get the bishop's attention, points his head at the big red seat next to him. The bishop has forgotten his place. Or he just wants to sit with the rest of us for a change.

This time the reading's about the desert breaking into song and flower. Daisy seems pleased to be reading.

The desert and the parched land will exult; the steppe will rejoice and bloom.

About the blind seeing and the deaf hearing, about the lame skipping and the mute finding their tongues, singing harmonies.

Then the eyes of the blind will be opened, the ears of the deaf be cleared.

Then will the lame leap like a stag, then the tongue of the dumb will sing.

It rings true about flowers in a desert, about anything growing. Streams and rivers bursting in the prairie, springs in the dry lands and up ahead a highway called the holy way.

It is for those with a journey to make, and on it the redeemed will walk.

MIKE

According to the order of service the first reading should have been from Ezekiel. I can see Father Pat's eyes widening. People start to murmur. It's unusual to have two readings from the Old Testament and neither of them the one in the program. Buster is looking behind him, frowning. Father Pat clears his throat a second time.

The bishop is pretty straight up about it. He's old, so I guess it's hard to keep track of everything all the time. "I was mixed up," he says. "Very sorry. Let's see. Here's the one." And he lets Daisy start this time.

This time nobody laughs, from the very back to the very front, they all fall silent, as if it is a book of prophecy she holds.

It's this reading about the miracle in the desert, everything blooming and rivers running where there aren't any before. The bishop was right to change it. Annie would have liked it. It was the kind of thing she believed in.

VERA

It isn't the reading in the program. None of them has been so far.

The first time it happens, Father Pat sticks his head up like a periscope, wheels it round and round like a distress signal on a lighthouse, alarmed no doubt by all the erotic verses, then sits back relieved when the bishop leaves the podium. But when Daisy starts to recite a different reading too, Father Pat stops her after the first line, taps her on the shoulder, whispers but forgets about the microphone, "This is not in the program."

Daisy whispers back, just as audibly: "There's an error in the program, Father. The bishop said."

And with that she turns back to the congregation, looks at the book and starts over. There is not much he can say. Like Daisy says, *The bishop said.* I have to pinch myself from laughing out loud. Father Pat slinks back down into his chair and presses his hands together again, stares at the red carpet in the sanctuary. The aisle and the sanctuary are the only places we could afford carpet of any kind.

Father Pat insisted on choosing the readings for the funeral. He was dogmatic about it. "The wake is for the people. Let them grieve. The funeral is a witness for the whole church."

He wanted it low-key, he told me — nothing to emphasize her oddness or draw attention to her peculiar gifts. But neither of us had counted on the bishop. I am watching Father Pat. One moment closing his eyes, trying to pray; the next pulling himself forward, his neck bunched up over his white collar, like a lion ready to pounce.

By some strange miracle, the psalm is the same as the program and Father Pat sits back, relieved.

Florence recites the cantor lines, while the rest of us sing the response.

God, you are my God,
for you I long
for you my soul is thirsting
My body pines for you
like a dry, weary land without water

The choir stands to lead the response.

I thirst for you, O God.

We say it over and over again.

ANNIE

Long have I yearned; it's been a lifetime of yearning. My body, my soul always in search. A piece of me missing even before they took my insides. Searching always, desperate to put the torn parts of me together again, the puzzle of who I am, the lost puzzle pieces: Maman, Papa, Nana, the spirit in the water. Is this what they call the Holy?

My being thirsts for you.

KRISTIAN

It's hard to tell about Kelsey with that choir robe she's got on. Those big flappy sleeves and pleats over her belly. She could be carrying twins for all I know or not pregnant at all.

Hey, she smiled at me.

Fuck, that makes me feel worse. I don't deserve any of it. I'm a land parched, lifeless, without water, holed up in that shack out back, cooking crank all day, tweaking, tweaking, tweaking, chilling out. I feel like that dude at the River Styx we read about in grade ten English, as I drive get-away cars in the middle of the night, picking up packages from the sides of ditches, throwing others in their place. Meeting these goons with grey and gloom around them shot through with orange sickly light. I don't like the way it makes me feel. Ferrying me and them to certain death. When I look in the mirror afterwards, that's the light I carry too. The light of despair and pain.

When Florence tries to recite the second reading from the book of Revelation, the bishop jumps up from where he's sitting, grabs his cane, hobbles up the risers and starts to add commentary that this passage is about the ancients' worship and belief in the fertility of the moon cycle, and, my God, you should see people's eyebrows shoot up. It's like he's got a gusher in him, that he's got to let out, and there's no stopping him.

On either side of the river grew the tree of life that produces fruit twelve times a year, once each month;...

"It's only womankind," he presses on, "who can potentially produce fruit twelve times a year. That, of all mammals, she can become pregnant any month of the year, that she isn't tied to instinct but a creature of choice!" The old coot is practically raving by this point. I glance over at Daisy; she looks like she's enjoying this too.

"The fruit of her womb," the bishop references the Virgin Mary and smiles up at Kelsey by way of example, "is a gift." He goes on commentating about how womankind are the font of life-giving waters, how they carry the tree of life in their bodies, and Annie was like the healing tree at the centre of the world whose leaves healed the nations. That he had known Annie's grandmother when she was alive, and she had told him that the witching worked best on the lunar cycle, and he had been scared of what he did not understand. But now that he is an old man, a lot he had believed seems foolish to him. How it is clear to him that it is all part of God's design.

Still, what the bishop says next is prin'near fantastical. How in the Old Testament the Wisdom of God is a woman, Sophia they called her in the Greek. How she was the Word that came forth from the mouth of God. Or some such madcap.

Come to think of it, Daisy is what I would call a wise woman. Might be something to that. Florence takes a deep breath and reads another line.

…the leaves of the trees serve as medicine for the nations.

DAISY

It is a fine reading, about the river of life, a much better reading than the one Father Pat ordered with all kinds of sternness about the end of the world. Still, more than a few of us think the behaviour of the bishop is peculiar. Those words about *Hagia Sophia,* Holy Wisdom, about her being the breath of God and covering the world like a mist. How she was there beside God at the creation of the universe, playing along with him, throwing in an opinion, and lending him a hand! I mean I have heard those readings before but I never knew what they meant. Afterwards, Florence leans over and says in my ear, "That was the gift of tongues."

VERA

I never thought in my lifetime I would hear the Word of women proclaimed from the altar by a man of the cloth.

FATHER PAT

I had purposely chosen Revelations 21, *I am the Alpha and the Omega, the beginning and the end,* to remind them who is the giver of life-giving water, he who is the giver of life. More important than any water in their fields.

To the thirsty I will give a gift from the spring of life-giving water.

Obviously the bishop's mind is affected. We agreed he would lead the service with me, but I am preaching. Here he is walking towards me with the book of the gospels, bowing, asking for a blessing.

"But Your Excellency?"

"Bless me, Father Pat," he whispers, "or the people will think we've mixed things up."

"But you have," I hiss.

"Thank you, Father." And with that he crosses himself and makes a small bow before he raises the green clothed book into the air and limps down in front of the altar to read the text. Kelsey hurries to steady him on the first step and hold the book for him. He seems to have thrown off his cane. He leans on her arm, and I find myself worrying for her, not wanting her to trip. I catch up to them, steady his bad side, while Kelsey turns the gold ribbon to the gospel.

ALEX

The bishop starts to tell the story.

Now that very day, two of them were going to a village seven miles from Jerusalem called Emmaus and they were conversing about all the things that had occurred. And it happened that while they were conversing and debating, Jesus himself drew near and walked with them, but their eyes were prevented from recognizing him.

"They didn't recognize Jesus, my dear people. I too failed to recognize him in his body, the church. This woman who has been living in your midst: Annie Gallagher. But you recognized her in the witching of the water. You recognized her as she sorted mail for you, as she brewed you a cup of coffee or poured you a beer at the end of a long day."

Were not our hearts burning [within us]...?

"Oh yes, our hearts were burning. Were they not?" Florence practically sings.

"Yes, Father," Bob calls out, then catches himself, slinks back into his seat, like he remembers we're not in a Baptist church here. But no one stares. They're all listening to the bishop and thinking pretty much the same thing, their mouths propped open.

The bishop beams. "Yes indeed!"

I can't help but think of the post office, the coffee nook, and the Table of Truth.

"Did she ever raise a word of complaint about her suffering? Do any of you know she was sent away from this place? To live where all the rejects of our society are sent. An institution. Those we thought were inhuman. And I'm ashamed to say that I was the main one who sent her.

"The Provincial Training School for Mental Defectives. That's what they called it in those days.

"Because her grandmother witched wells and Annie saw and understood things beyond her years and because Annie held herself with a particular grace. God help me, she was beautiful!" He said it without any hint of apology. And then more somberly, suddenly near tears, "She was 'sent away' my dear people, because I lusted after her."

The church falls silent as a tomb. No one moves, spellbound by the spectacle of the bishop, fallen to his knees at the top of the risers, heaving. A minute, then two, passes and he pushes himself up on his cane with both hands to keep going.

"What the women had to say astounded the apostles and astounds us! They have been faithful friends, these women who have prepared the body, prepared the ceremony today, because they know that Annie was with us, she is with us, and she will rise at the last day.

With that their eyes were opened and they recognized him, but he vanished from their sight.

"Your eyes were opened long before mine, in the water. It was only these past hours that my own eyes were opened, and I recognized her.

Were not our hearts burning [within us] while he spoke to us on the way and opened the scriptures to us?

"Did not our hearts burn as she explained the Book of Creation to us?"

People speak up one after another. The Mueller boy, Kristian, in the front row, nods his head like a nervous jack rabbit this time.

"I lost track of Annie. The good women of your community have told me what happened." He points out Daisy and Florence and Vera.

"She ran away from the training school, ended up in the city, on skid row. After that institution, Annie was never able to have children. She took up drinking. That was all more than six decades ago. And I feel God's redemption speaking powerfully through your presence here today.

"When she found her way home, she found her father had fallen onto hard times. She stayed to help him with his work. She continued to drink. When he died, she drank more.

"It is the women who are at the tomb first. 'Some women from our group...' Some women who had received the mystery. But their story seemed like *'nonsense'* to the apostles. Can we believe them? Peter has to go see for himself.

"After his death, Jesus does *not* go up to Jerusalem or any other places of power or centres of economy. He does not appear in a temple or a synagogue or a church or on the steps of city hall. No, he appears at a table with friends, in a garden with his beloved, on a country road to two travellers. All these common places we occupy in our daily lives. And he never looks like we expect but is completely recognizable.

"In Luke he is made known to them in the breaking of the bread. In John it's in the sharing of a fresh-caught fish. It could have been anything lifegiving. To hunger, to thirst: these are human. To feed, to quench, to show compassion, this is the work of the Christian. In Jewish tradition every meal is opened with a ritual blessing of bread.

"My dear people, it doesn't much matter what is shared. It is in the act of sharing that we recognized her."

He's right on that point. It doesn't much matter what. A word, a feeling, touch. A meal. That's probably the thing I miss most about not having someone in my life. Someone to share the worrying window with. Your day can start out like hell. You can journey, journey, and journey through, but if you don't have someone to share a meal with at the end and make sense of it, it's all just a maze.

VERA

"She was struck down," the bishop pauses for emphasis, "doing a work of mercy for a neighbour. For we were thirsty and she gave us drink!"

Heads are nodding all over the church.

One young man is sobbing with his head in his hands, sobbing and shaking like a leaf. The same one I saw at the wake. Before the service I asked Mike if he knew him. The only face I don't know. "Trouble," he said. "Hans Mueller's son."

Kelsey — who was living with Annie, Florence's taken her in now — is watching him too. Her eyes are welling up. She keeps trying to dab at them with her wide sleeve.

Trouble? Now don't tell me that's her young man?

I remember Hans and Kristian now from their visits to the hospital when Mrs. Mueller took sick. He has grown two feet since then.

"When lightning struck Annie, death would have been near instantaneous. A split second of suffering and she would have been free."

The young man looks up from his crying, an expression of disbelief on his face, just like a new puppy, miserable one moment, happy the next. His hands grab the pew in front of him, push Rita Chambers' sweater out of the way, and he shakes his curly brown hair back out of his eyes. They are bloodshot and ringed with sleep-lessness. Trouble. I've seen that look enough at the Emerg. For a minute I think he's going to get up and shout something out too. But instead the bishop speaks.

"Annie was a work of mercy. She took in a young girl that needed a home. She was hungry and Annie gave her food. She was naked and Annie clothed her. Annie was a power for good."

And that is partly where the idea takes hold in this new way that Annie was special, like some of us thought, but he is the first to say it out loud.

"Blessed," he says. "She *is* blessed."

And this lends credence to the notion that she is on the first leg of the road to sainthood.

KRISTIAN

First the bishop says that thing about the lightning and then I hear her speak. I'll never forget that voice.

Kristian, you want the good. Follow where it takes you. And I realize the colour I am seeing around her coffin. The colour green. Green puts me in mind of earth, of fields, and I feel a sudden calm strung on a line through my head, down my gut to the heels of my feet, all the twisting gone inside and out. All the pieces of me fitting together again. And I want to weep for joy, but I don't deserve it, I almost say out loud, when the big guy sitting behind me, the same one I saw at the wake and again this morning, gives me another pat on the back and tells me, "All will be right."

ANNIE

People's eyes bug out of their heads. Someone clears his throat. No one's ever told them the unvarnished truth before from the pulpit. The place has run quiet. The young priest's neck rises, his mouth gapes open like a gander on full territorial display.

It took half my life to get over my anger. As soon as the bishop makes his peace, I let go my body. Shuck it off, permeate the air in this place.

This is what I can say of the time I was taken. My mother had gone away when I was very small. No one said how or why till much later. My father on his death bed told me how her father was a town administrator, how they lived in a comfortable villa near the border, how her parents were shot by the advancing German army at the start of the war, the village burned to the ground. How her sister stayed with the German soldier who had taken them in and protected them. How Francesca had to cross the line alone.

She and my father had fallen in love and married quick-like as people did in those days, thinking that they were about to die. And I came just at the beginning of their new life in this land, which was the best thing that could have happened.

He had been selfish to woo her and bring her back. She had grown up with comforts he could never give her. He recollected how she had watched at the window every day, except in the heat of summer. Then she might be outside for a few minutes. But if a breeze stirred she would say "I feel chilled" and want to go inside. She left off eating, and feeding me, too. My father started to come home at noon rather than eating dinner with his men at midday and would try to feed us both in his fumbling way. My nana lived across the street, and she began to spend evenings with us and cook our suppers.

By the end of her time with us, Maman was as thin as a ghost, and she disappeared, as my nana used to say, into thin air.

This was when I started to live between my father's house and my grandmother's and where I first learned how to name the waters in me and the other bodily humours. My nana told me about the moon's power and its cycles in a woman's body. She showed me how to listen for the water. Told me how it was a gift in our family, how when all else failed – we could live by witching.

My nana saw me raised a Catholic, my first confession, my first communion, confirmation. I memorized all the questions Sister Aloysius read out of that blue and white book they called the Baltimore Catechism.

Who is God?

What is man?

What must we do to save our souls?

And I memorized all the answers because the words came up backwards for me on the page. It took me longer to understand what others were seeing; it took me longer to read.

I turned eight the first year of the Great Depression, though no one knew what it was at first. The banks were starting to fail and people couldn't get credit. The next year the drought came and the crops failed too. There wasn't much call for bricks and my father thought it best we make a change. People wouldn't build when there was no money, but they needed a place to be with friends. That is when he started on the hotel.

All this time, I know now, the powers that be were growing in their interest in me, watching me fill out, suspicious of my sprouting breasts and my rounding hips, of my face that was lengthening, sharpening into focus like my mother's so that when my nana died in her sleep, and I reached the cusp of womanhood, they took me for my own good, they said. Took me from out of a corrupting influence, a hotel and a young girl living alone with her father. No place for a growing girl who even the teachers said was in need of special training.

15

FLORENCE

A big silence envelops the church as the young Father takes the bucket from its place by the altar, walks down the centre aisle and round and round the casket sprinkling it three times three, sprinkling the holy water on her casket and all of us praying, so powerfully silent. Till he nods at the choir that it is time to go.

He sings, "Into the womb of God, we commend our sister, Annie. May this water of life speed her on her journey."

He stares down at the place where the words leave his mouth, where his breath meets air. The young priest can't seem to stop himself. The words keep coming out at odds with what he has planned.

"Carry her on her way! Great rainclouds full. Thunderheads."

There's surprise in his eyes. I call that Godsmacked.

"This holy water blessed by the church, by nature, a meeting of waters, waters above and below. Bring her to your bosom. Remind her of her origins."

"What did I tell you? The power of the water," I say to no one in particular.

All of a sudden the front doors blow open.

JACK

I swear I see her rising. For a split second. Annie pulling herself up from her coffin, her white hair rippling around her. It might be a trick of the light, an old man's vision and the view up here in the choir loft. The way the beams of sunlight shiver over her face.

ANNIE

This is how I was taken. It was a Sunday afternoon in spring. Pubs were always closed on Sundays then, and there were no guests staying at the hotel that weekend, so we were home. My father was dozing on the couch; he had been drinking whisky the day they came, as he had more and more since Maman had left and Nana was gone.

I had attended church on my own as I was wont to do after my nana died. Washed and dressed myself as best I could that morning, tried to go to confession before mass and take communion. But it was no good. I was growing out of everything. Dresses were tight across the chest, my good shoes pinched. Father Leo was curt with me in the confessional before mass, sharp even. He insisted I was lying to him. "You are guilty of the sin of omission," he said. I shook my head; I didn't understand. It was not enough to say I had talked back to my father, that I had called someone at school a name, that I had shoved a boy that week who had teased me. Father Leo refused to absolve me or give me communion that day.

Four of them came to the house: the young doctor from one town over with his leather medical bag; my teacher, Mrs. Burke, from school; one of the ladies from church, also a member of the United Farm Women; and young Father Leo.

I was in the backyard pruning the roses, clearing out the brambles from the raspberry patch, turning the vegetable garden with a spade so that we could plant that year. I had been taught how to tend all of it. I had on a pair of my father's old jeans. Each leg rolled up to my ankles, cinched tight on the waist, and an old plaid shirt of his with the sleeves cut down. He wanted me to wear Nana's clothes, but she had been a completely different shape than me, elongated as she was like a string bean. My father was long too but with heft to the shoulders and a waist closer to my own.

They had knocked long and loud, till finally I had to come around from the back to let them in. They did not wipe their feet. They did not remove their hats or sit down. They looked angry, indignant, righteous. I thought they had come to give my father a lecture. But they motioned for me to step inside too and closed the door. My father stirred, cracked open one eye, saw the black Model B Ford of the RCMP parked outside, sat up as straight as a robin in a field, and tried to pull himself to his feet but his legs betrayed him. The two women stood by me; Mrs. Burke tried to pat my shoulder, but I shook off her touch. The doctor took up a position in the passageway to the kitchen; Father Leo blocked the front door. One by one they stood over him till he signed the order. And on it were listed the reasons for my removal:

Truancy

Unkempt appearance

A minor in a public house

Public drunkenness in a guardian

Immoral behaviour between father and daughter.

It was true after my nana had died there was no one to make sure I took a bath, combed my hair, washed and mended my clothes. It was true I helped my father at the hotel some evenings, but no one had ever bothered me. They knew I was Declan Gallagher's daughter. It was true I had been kept back a grade that year. Nana wasn't there to help me with my reading, and I missed her in ways I cannot tell.

It was true about my father's drinking. But it was the accusation of incest that sealed it for the doctor. He made notes, nodded to the others.

"Father Leo," I said, trying to rush to him. The doctor and the two women grabbed my arms and held me back. "Stop them! Tell them! There's no truth to the last. You know that."

"But I don't know that, my child. I don't." His eyes flashed. "Living alone with this man. And you the temptation of Eve." He clenched and unclenched his fists. "I have a responsibility to see that you grow into womanhood uncorrupted." He turned away from me then, and opened the front door to the waiting officers.

"Papa!" I sobbed.

My father tried to rise again, his face flushed, breathing hard: "I've never touched my Annie. I've never..." but the drink was too much in him.

They took me as I was: brambles in my hair, an old cut off pair of rubber boots on my feet, a shirt torn on one sleeve where the thorns had caught. They told my father they would just burn my clothes at the institution anyway, and that there was no sense throwing good after bad.

I fought them: I scratched, I kicked. When I bit one of the officers in the arm, the doctor took out the straitjacket. It took three men to bind me: my arms wrenched into the sleeves, crossed and pulled tight over my chest and cinched. After three hours in the back seat of the car, my elbows were swollen, my hands were numb, and I was screaming for release.

"Don't fight," one of the officers said to me. "You only make it worse."

BUSTER

The door blows open and all hell breaks loose on earth or heaven, however you see it. As soon the wind starts to stir up the proceedings, I start to laugh out loud. And that old bugger talking off the cuff like that. All the ladies and the priests trying to keep their skirts in place. The choir clutching their sheet music, such as it is, to their breasts. Little picture cards of Annie with her obituary on the back tear out of hymnals, out of hands, blow up and out of the open windows. Some of us try to hang on to our folding chairs. I can feel her plain as day. Irascible. "That would be Annie," I yell back at Jack. He just nods and smiles. Alex and Mike are ushering today, so it's their job to plough through the mob and get the door shut.

The young Mueller fellow in front of us is finally enjoying himself. He's on his feet cheering and waving both arms in the air. Around the church, people reach to slam down any casement that is handy to them. I say to Bob who is sitting next to me in the pew, "I reckon we're about to get a tornado."

"Better find the basement," he says to me, but neither of us moves.

ANNIE

I still grow the *fève* in the back garden. Nana saved the seed from that first generation in the new land. We sowed them every year after she left. A row for Maman. They are still flowering, putting forth seed, seeking, rising to meet the light.

Do you or I or anyone know how oats, beans and barley grow?

My father didn't know that it was any one thing. The shock of the mud road. The two-room wood frame house. The wide flat plains. The sudden vicious thunderstorms. The cold. A new language in a strange place.

There were no books, no music. The closest thing to an instrument, a fiddle that he couldn't play.

The women were suspicious of her; her beauty looked exotic to them.

At first, the nuns from Victoire visited and spoke to my mother in their slurred and guttural Quebecois, an old French gnarled by harsh winters. My father said they tried to cheer her up, urge her to adapt to the snow, to the empty land, the new language.

They should have known it can take generations to adapt a people, my father said, but they were innocent women without knowledge of evil. My mother had lived through war.

My father said she was almost giddy with expectation waiting for me to be born, but some days after she had me, he found her by my crib clasping and unclasping her hands, my diapers full, crying to be held, to be fed. As I grew, her mood swings took on a quieter temper.

She tried to make croissants, kneaded, rolled in butter, then kneaded a second time, but it was hard to get the dough right. She complained the flour here was too coarse, the butter too thin. She spent hours in the kitchen, her dresses streaked with flour and oil, and by the end of it, she was in tears.

She tried to garden, but the tomatoes and the cucumbers almost always froze. There was never enough water for the squash, never enough heat for the eggplants and the sweet peppers. Finally she gave up on gardening except for the fava bean, *le fève,* the one thing that came out all right. She would fry them in butter, fresh. The only thing she would eat some days, sitting in front of the house's largest window, straight out of the pan with a wooden spoon. I remember near the end, her reaching down, the wooden spoon, the fresh green fava bean. She would spoon it right into my mouth.

I'm not sure how to paint what happens next. Maybe like old prayer cards. A light coming through the roof. A dove overhead. A tongue of fire. Maybe the lightning bolt that found Annie has followed her here to this place, has split the mind of the old man in two. Even the young priest is too overtaken to protest. Maybe this is a mini-Pentecost what we're having, all jammed into this place, expecting a visitation, expecting Jesus, and walking out with tongues of fire over our heads, babbling in strange languages instead.

The whir of winds came through like a heavenly rock and roll band, all bass and drums and a lead singer that was telling a hard truth in an even harder blasting tone. Others heard opera and old Jack said he heard country. Somebody else said it was in another language: Latin or what they imagined to be Greek. Doesn't matter, we all heard the music. Yet when the doors and the windows were finally shut and the overhead fans kicked off, it was gone.

The young Mueller boy was so overcome he was weeping practically through the whole service, shaking in his seat. I didn't even realize he knew Annie. Just goes to show the kind of effect she could have on people. The kid didn't let up till the bishop's homily and then he straightened up his shoulders, wiped his face with the back of his sleeve, and made eyes with the altar girl. Servers, I guess they call them nowadays. She seemed pretty happy about that and started weeping like women do when they're overcome with emotion.

"It's the wind," someone says.

And such a wind as I've ever seen in that church, lifts the cross laid on the pall, lifts the book of gospels, opens it, plays with the pages, before it's swept aside. Lifts the pall off the casket like a white cloud.

The wind whips through the church, raising handkerchiefs, mourners' hats, orders of service. Hymn books slam shut. Funeral cards whirl through the air.

The two priests clutch at their vestments, try to hold their cassocks below their knees. Father Pat loses the stole from around his neck. The mitre topples off the bishop's head and rolls on its side down the steps.

The sound of laughter and then she is gone.

"The Son of Man, lifted in glory," someone cries.

"May the Angels of God lead you to the Holy House of Wisdom." The old bishop is crying, his face jubilant, his robes whipping around him. "May Jesus, Child of Wisdom, welcome you to his table, heaped and ready for feasting!" The young priest looks terrified. "May they lay you down by Wisdom's streams and give you rest."

"Yes, come holy angels!" Florence prays.

Mrs. Cummins opens her mouth and sings a solo, she who has never sung a word in her life. A simple run up and down the C chord, a kind of improvised chant on "Alleluia," still, the rest of the choir looks giddy.

"Journey with her and stand beside her in the presence of the Holy Most Wide!" calls the bishop.

I let out a laugh. The pallbearers scramble to get the cloth back on top of her, to retrieve the gospels and the cross, but the wind won't let them. It's all they can do to keep the white pall on.

It takes Buster to yell, "Close the damn door!"

Mike and Alex have to climb through several lines of mourners, standing room only. Mike acts as the anchor, the two of them clasp hands to keep from blowing outside. The mourners who were on the steps have found shelter in their cars. Alex leans out from the ledge, pauses there as if he's getting a good look at the storm, smiles at something, then finally grabs the handle and gives it a good pull. Makes sure it's latched.

Inside the church, all falls still. The air is itself again. No one says anything for several seconds. No one moves. It was as if they sensed it too, the great rushing in of the Spirit. The bishop is on his knees, the young priest beside him, looking suddenly repentant and small, like those children at Lourdes in the holy pictures you see.

JACK

Kelsey flips the pages of the big red book trying to find the right passage — all the pages and the ribbon markers blown aside in the gust. Finally Father Pat settles on a prayer from memory and inspiration.

"To you, O God of Mystery, we commend our sister, Annie."

An old one rejigged.

"In the hope that we who have lived by the breath of your Word, manifest in this land, will join you in the presence of Wisdom at that feast of great peace."

Another strange reference. And those of us who think that is the end of it, have already started to utter Amen, when the young priest goes on in spite of himself.

"We give thanks for the blessings which you gave us through Annie in her lifetime, for her gift of witching."

Heads are nodding. I'm embarrassed for him.

"Urr — finding water. For her gifts of healing and gathering of community."

The young priest takes a step back, looks down at his breath, starts to claw the air, his fists trying to push the words back into his mouth. But they keep on.

"We are truly grateful. Take our sister, Annie, to her place of rest."

"A case of possession if I've ever seen one," Buster comments in a loud voice.

Then the bishop starts to sing.

May the sun and moon and stars and all the angels and saints rise to meet her.

Oh yes, God, the angels, the wood nymphs, the tree spirits.

May this water,

Drawn from the river of life,

May this water speed her on her journey.

The bishop exchanges branch and water bucket for the incensor again.

May this fragrance of ancient wood and bloom

carry her into your garden!

The choir rises to attention, croaks the lines:

Holy saints journey with her!

Sing her passage, angels of God.

Surround her in beauty, Bright Morning Star!

And stand beside her in the presence of the Creator most holy.

FATHER PAT

"Yes, may the angels lead you."

I look over. It is the bishop, fervent, on his knees, and on the other side, the choir accompanying him a cappella on the final farewell.

May the angels lead you to Wisdom's feast.

Mrs. Cummins takes a stab at accompaniment of the chant, on the right hand, key of C, one note, D. And the choir knows the words and the melody to a chant that's never been sung before.

ALEX

And guess what is standing on the threshold of the church when I go to close the door? A magpie. Maybe one of those in the school-yard the other night. Or maybe someone I know?

"Annie?" I say quietly. The bird cocks its head and hops a ways away and takes off. I decide, right then and there, I'm going to put my mug up on an online dating site.

Only then I notice the guy with the Christopher medal high-tailing it down to the shiny black suv parked at the foot of the hill, every few steps looking back at me, his face white as a sheet. I let out a good belly laugh, get hold of the door handle and give it a good tug shut.

ANNIE

When my father made bricks, sometimes he used wood instead of coal, wood taken as its sap was rising, eight-foot cordwood, the smell of that wood, cured. When I would go to sleep, the smell all around me on my bed at night, when I would rise for school the next morning. Our house was next door to the brickworks, scove ovens, the shape of oversized bread loaves, always a stack, and sometimes a sweet smell, the smell of honey, I fancied. I knew my father was up off and on in the night checking the fire, watching the bricks turn colour and I felt protected.

Before the war, his father had been the town smithy. That was where he learned about the temperatures of fire and the heat needed to turn steel and iron; the colours of the coals and what to watch for; the right fuel for the right temperature. When to use bellows, when to turn the blade, when to hammer the birthing iron. Tongs for different-sized pieces. How to fix harrows and plough-shares, to shoe a horse, to mend a harness. That's why they had him work with the horses.

I wasn't allowed near the fires on my own. A week after my mother left, my father showed me the mouth of the furnace, the coals were like white crystal at the centre, hardly any orange or yellow, even at the edges.

"This is a vision of paradise," he told me.

"The colour of fire?" I asked, uncertain.

"The wonder of things changing from one substance to another: from soft to firm, from green to matured. The force it takes to create anything. To grow a human being."

I did not understand it then, but let the clear diamond of it rest in my eye and thought of it often when I was sent away. What the clay must endure to come out a useful building material, strong and lasting, able to survive even the fire that brought it into being.

"That brick," said my father, having survived hell once himself, "emptied of all its impurities, can never be destroyed."

Later, when he was dying, he told me something changed for him, when he saw fire used to kill man and beast. There were days he would pray for snow. Or drink.

He looked forward to the winter on the front. Yes it was cold, but the snow would harden the earth, make the hauling smoother, the going easier. The snow made everything bearable, erased memory of broken bodies — human, horse, machine. Made a blank canvas. Made a dream canvas.

That and the whisky kept him sane. This is how it began: he gave the horse whisky for colic. It settled her. He took a nip; it settled him. Indigestion of any sort, of the body or the mind.

But what he pressed down, what he kept from thought, the weight that sank in the heart, rose double after the war. At first it was only at night, to keep the nightmares at bay, he said. A nip and a swallow. But then it grew, came unbidden, at any time, day or night, alone or in company. Each loss made it worse. The loss of his wife, my mother. The death of his own mother. The loss of his young daughter and the return of her, so changed. Most of all, the knowledge that he couldn't protect me.

He begged my forgiveness.

BUSTER

The old fellow has the incensor — he sent the altar girl back for it — and he starts dancing around the casket with it. People cheer and clap. The old man starts to laugh.

That's when the young priest rushes up to him.

"Your Grace. Get a hold of yourself," he says.

The bishop doesn't mince words. "You're so much like me when I was your age. Righteous and scared to death."

You should see the young priest's face. But the old guy isn't finished.

"With any luck and the grace of God, you'll grow out of it."

That's when he hands Kelsey the incensor, waves his arms to quiet everyone down and makes the announcement.

"The deconsecration is off!"

"It's a miracle!" someone exclaims.

Mrs. Cummins falls to her knees. And the choir starts to chant *Lord have mercy,* all of us following on. *Christ have mercy,* and we repeat. *Lord have mercy,* quite obediently. Vera starts to call out obscure names, women, all of them as near as I can figure. Daisy tells me they're old saints and martyrs, not often feted, all women you only hear about in the middle of the night at Easter, if you hear about them at all.

Saint Mary Magdalene, watch over us.

Saint Agatha, watch over us.

Saint Lucy, watch over us.

Saint Agnes, watch over us.

Daisy says they've stared down lions, emperors, popes, religious orders (same thing when you think about it). Wrestled with beasts, resisted rape, lost their breasts for their convictions. Studied the scriptures. (Daisy's used to translating for me after all these years so's that I can follow the confusing rituals these Catholics have at times.)

Catherine of Alexandria, counsel us.

Saint Anastasia...

Saint Teresa of Avila...

Inspired music, poetry. Sailed ships and seas. Filled a lake with beer (well, that sounds mighty good).

Saint Cecilia, journey with us.

Saint Ursula...

Saint Brighid...

A whole line of them, one after another and the choir singing in between. Just one of the schemes the women had gotten up to. A litany she called it. A kind of singing home. Pretty thing. I squeeze her shoulder affectionate-like.

MIKE

And then when the old bishop made that announcement that he was not going to close the church, we were all on our feet in a second. Clapping and cheering, people were whistling, throwing their hats in the air. It was a silly time. Pure nonsense, but wasn't that what they taught us in catechism was a sign of the Spirit?

Thelma Cummins was so taken up that she sang a solo, a song no one knew in these parts and there just wasn't any explanation other than divine intervention. No one knew she could even sing.

That's when Florence revealed that she had been praying to Annie for a sign, an intervention, and God was great and the Virgin Mary Ever So Holy. And this was Annie's first miracle on the road to sainthood.

DAISY

Florence said it was the gift of tongues but I understood every word.

ANNIE

Maman left my father a letter. I found it years later at the bottom of his chest of drawers, in an old cigar box. It was in childish script and in French; this is my best translation.

> We were *domestiques*, my sister and I. Our master was the town administrator. His mistress was good to us. She let us grow the *fève* through the war and we had kept up the garden even after they were gone. It kept us alive during the war. I'd never been to school unless you count the time in Paris when I tried to teach myself by reading the newspapers. We were orphans. Our mother died when

I was born. Our father was killed in a mining accident. We had no land. My sister raised me.

Almond trees grew on some estates, but I'd never seen an orange tree or a lemon. Only pictures in magazines some of the soldiers brought with them. Nor had I ever eaten olives, until I got to Paris. I had never been outside of my region before the war.

I was from Nancy, from Paris, from Marseilles, from everywhere, changing my identity to fit the need. That was the way it was during the war. We told lies, my sister and I. Place to place, before the war and through it. Survival depended on stories and the *fève*. The *fève* — my sister and I lived off the *fève*. It was our salvation. Wherever we lived we were allowed to plant a few rows for our own use. It was the only thing all those years that was ours.

We didn't hide in a cellar and watch the village burn around us though I'd heard of others who did. When the village was taken by the Germans, we let ourselves be taken. When the Allies retook our village, I hid until I thought it was safe to come out. It is true my sister slept with a German officer and stayed with him as his mistress. I dreamed of going south, where there was no war. My sister did not want me to leave.

I crossed the line early that morning at Verdun. I was on the road to Paris, to the theatre, where I'd heard they took any girls who could sing or dance, especially girls from the provinces, and made them into chorus girls, and some, into courtesans for the soldiers. That there was a good living in it.

When I met you for the first time, I had just stood aside to let the convoys pass. I was standing in front of an *estaminet*. You thought I worked there as a serving girl; I never corrected you. That one brilliant evening made me forget for a few brief moments everything I had lost or had never had. I watched the troops move up the line, feeling ecstatic and grim in the same body. Longing for a home and the end of the war and my sister who I never saw again.

I almost left you twice before. Once on the docks at London before joining the queue with the other women. Soldiers and war brides were shipped then by separate passage, and you had already gone ahead. I went to brush my hair in the ladies lavatory. I had two pounds in my purse. I could lose myself in the crowds, catch the boat going back to the continent where I'd come from. But then I remembered. Whole cities, villages were in ruins. There was nothing to go back to.

The other time was on the other side of the ocean, alone, at the port in Montreal. I almost melted away into the crowds, carried along in the opposite direction by the strange but familiar language of the passersby, but I kept thinking about your goodness and how you had saved me from a life of dissolution. I still had hope in the future.

And *pour ma fille*. There were days you won't remember, when you were walking already. I'd feed you and put us both back to bed. Sleep was my only escape. When you couldn't sleep anymore, I took to sitting in the window. I had to save myself. I didn't worry about you. You were a child of this place. The soil, already in you. You had your grandmother and your father. I had nothing left to give. My story was wearing thin.

The bishop has to do the dismissal, and he's almost out of breath.

"May the One who is Mystery bless us."

Everyone bows their heads, starts to make the sign on their forehead, on their heart, on their shoulders.

"Go in peace. In the friendship of our God, the Three-in-One."

"Amen. Amen." Everyone says it twice, without noticing, like the Evangelicals do all the time, echoing on itself, but it was that kind of service.

ANNIE

Florence gathers up the book and the cross, up they lift me, surprised some of them at how light I've become, how light this body feels, all the water gone out of me into the air, into the ground. People are looking up, pointing at the first soft patter on the roof. And now a roaring, a downpour.

For the procession out of the church, they shoulder me like they still do in the countryside sometimes where people are used to working with their bodies, still used to lifting dead weight. Down the steps and across the lawn to the cemetery on the eastern side. A few pull out their umbrellas, at least to keep the books dry. But most are so overcome by the taste of rain that they slosh like children again through the growing puddles.

The choir recites: *May the angels lead you into the arms of Holy Wisdom; may the martyrs journey with you to that place of great peace!*

Down the aisle we follow, all of us singing, *Amazing Grace,* in three parts.

That must be the Lutherans, Mrs. Cummins murmurs to the lady next to her. The only ones who can be counted on to carry a tune in these parts and sing all the verses.

"Well this is surely the best funeral this church has ever seen," another lady says.

The choir continues its impromptu hymn: *May the angels welcome you to Wisdom's feast, where the lowly and the lofty eat and drink at the same table, where pain and sorrow shall be no more, where Love makes her home.*

And the doors fly open again and the wind and the rain swallow us as we march to the cemetery.

ACKNOWLEDGEMENTS

I like to say it takes a community to write a book.

I spent many hours at the Provincial Archives of Alberta poring over original documents from the Red Deer Provincial Training School for Mental Defectives, which was transformed into Michener Centre in 1977. I interviewed two former staff of the Centre in 2009 and 2010: Norma Martin about her experience as a special education teacher at the training school starting in 1963 and Anita Jenkins about her summer job there in the early sixties. All of these sources helped me imagine some of the scenes in the book.

Local military historian Maurice Doll helped steer me in the right direction in my World War I research. J. Frank Henderson. liturgist and good friend, dissected the litany form for me.

Several people helped me understand the western grain elevator, among them Hans Huizinga of the Alberta Grain Elevator Society, my uncle Alfred Schermann who used to work on the railroad and witnessed at least one demolition, and Jim A. Pearson, author of *Vanishing Sentinels*.

Civil servants from Alberta Agriculture and Forestry answered my many questions about historical and contemporary crop rotation techniques, while Matt Haisan, family friend and farmer, was generous in sharing his love and lore of the farming life.

Any factual errors that remain are my own.

I am grateful to Banff Centre (both the Leighton Studios and the former Self-directed Residency Program) and the Sage Hill Writing Experience for quiet places to retreat and to write and to each of Lawrence Hill and Helen Humphrey for their unique editorial expertise and encouragement. I remain indebted to the book's first readers who were cheering and incisive in equal measure: Anita Jenkins, Astrid Blodgett, Fran Kimmel, and Julie Robinson. I first discussed the idea for this book with Jacqueline Baker, whose enthusiasm was unequivocal. I thank the Edmonton Arts Council and the Alberta Foundation for the Arts for funding the retreats and editorial consultations for this book.

It has been a pleasure to work with the team at NeWest Press in Edmonton: Matt Bowes for his enthusiasm and support for the book from the outset; Claire Kelly for her editing, marketing and organizational skills; and Douglas Barbour for his editorial guidance, par excellence.

Thank you.